Aldo Moon

and the
Ghost at Gravewood Hall

First published in Great Britain by Scribo MMXIII
Scribo, a division of Book House, an imprint of
The Salariya Book Company
25 Marlborough Place, Brighton, BN1 1UB
www.salariya.com

Text Copyright © Alex Woolf MMXIII
ISBN 978-1-908177-84-1

The right of Alex Woolf to be identified as the author of this
work has been asserted in accordance with sections 77 and 78
of the Copyright, Designs and Patents Act, 1988.

Book Design by David Salariya

© The Salariya Book Company
and Bailey Publishing Associates MMXIII

Printed and bound in India.
Reprinted in MMXIV.

The text for this book is set in Cochin.
The display type is Rough Riders.

www.scribobooks.com

Aldo Moon

and the Ghost at Gravewood Hall

ALEX WOOLF

SCRIBO

A division of Book House

2014004 054

WINTERBY VILLAGE

School

Meadow

to Hertford

to Ware

Richard Culpin's House

Wood Shed

Stable Block

GRAVEWOOD HALL

GROUND FLOOR

Rear Garden

Morning Room | Library

Rear Parlour | Study

Drawing Room | Dining Room

Lawn

Church

Mound

Old Cock Inn

Winterby Woods

to Harlow

Apothecary

to Hoddesdon

Butcher

Wheelwright

Gravewood Hall

to London

Blacksmith

KEY
■ Ghostly sighting
▲ Possible ghostly sighting

4

CHAPTER

I

'It was a dark and stormy night,' I began. 'The skies were racked by thunder that rolled in waves across the valley. Lightning forked through the dismal clouds and lit up the trees in brief, angry flashes.'

Actually, it was a beautiful evening. The only celestial illumination was provided by the moon, which shone through wisps of London fog, falling silkily upon our rug. But that didn't seem right for my story, which was to be in the Gothic tradition and so required a more violent kind of weather.

Aldo watched me, an amused expression at play on his lean, angular face. I had hoped for at least a pretence of excitement, but was grateful that he wasn't yet bored. I tried not to let his appearance put me off my stride. He looked ridiculous, as usual, in canary yellow trousers and turquoise waistcoat, with mermaids embroidered on the front. His baggy pirate shirt had lace frill cuffs that he twisted in his long, restless fingers. His hair was as dark and unruly as the storm I was trying to describe.

'The wind,' I said, 'was howling through the trees.'

'Doesn't it always!' groaned my cousin Lily, the third person in the room.

'Nothing in this universe, my dear girl, is so predictable that one can say it will *always* be so,' said Aldo. 'Although Nathan's stories may yet prove the exception.'

'You mean he won't ever surprise us?'

'I fear not.'

'Excuse me!' I interrupted. 'I'm trying to conjure an atmosphere here.'

'Well, how about conjuring some characters and a plot?' said the heartless Lily.

We were in the sitting room of our home in St John's Wood, London, the three of us, passing the time before bed by telling stories. I slowly paced the rug in front of the fireplace, hoping for inspiration, and feeling a little irked at my audience's lack of appreciation so far. I had grown up on a diet of popular adventure stories, read to me by my father, and their legacy was a head full of over the top description. Rain always fell in torrents, blood always boiled and girls' eyes were never anything but meltingly blue. It's not the way I speak normally, you understand. Normally I'm as restrained as the next fellow. But ask me for a story and I'll offer up enough wooden phrases to build a fleet of ships. I simply cannot help it.

Lily was perched on a sofa on the far side of the room from Aldo. She was a pretty girl, I always thought, although she did not seem to think herself so, and made every effort to be plain. Her dark curls were pinned tightly back, exposing her ears. Her high-collared dress, with its vertical strip of buttons, went almost up to her chin. The result was a severity of appearance that even the cheerful glow from the fireplace could do little to mellow. She had ambitions to be a scientist, but she looked more like a strict governess to a bunch of rowdy young boys.

They waited, none too hopefully, for the continuation of my tale.

'The clouds,' I said to them, 'were racing across the sky, and the rain... the rain was lashing at the windows of the rickety old house in the woods.'

'I think that's quite enough about the weather, don't you?' said Lily, not even bothering to stifle her yawn. 'Now please get on with the story, Nathan Carter, or I shall be forced to go to bed.'

Lily was just sixteen, a full year younger than myself, and a mere girl, yet these facts did nothing to curb her tendency to mock and disparage me at every opportunity. She believed herself my superior in most things, and certainly in breeding. You see, although we were first cousins, Lily and I, her mother – my father's sister – had married into the Morelles, an ancient Anglo-Norman family that traced itself back to the time of William the Conqueror.

Both her parents were now dead, and Lily had been living here under the guardianship of my father since she was ten, yet she retained a condescending air of superiority, especially with me. She could send me into such a rage when she wanted to. Indeed, if she hadn't been a girl, and a relative, I'm afraid there were occasions when I could cheerfully have clobbered her. Even now I could feel my muscles tensing and the heat rising beneath my collar, and it took considerable effort to maintain my composure.

'Kindly stop your continual interruptions, cousin,' I barked. 'You have utterly ruined my flow.'

'I believe someone is about to knock,' Aldo suddenly announced.

'Thank you, Aldo,' I grimaced. 'Yes. Someone is indeed about to knock at the door of the rickety old house in the woods.'

'No, dear brother, you misunderstand,' he interrupted. 'I mean to say that I have picked up a ripple in the ether. I sense a change in the weather – in the cosmic weather, I mean. Someone is about to knock at the front door of this house, and this knock, I fear, will have grave consequences for all of us.'

'You're a fraud and a charlatan, Aldo Moon,' said Lily crossly. 'You heard a carriage pull up in the street.'

The sounds of the street would have had to carry up the staircase and through at least three walls if they were to reach us here in the parlour – surely beyond the range of any human ear. Lily knew this as well as I, yet she would sooner be rolled in marmalade and dangled in front of a nest of angry wasps than admit that Aldo had *actually* picked up anything in the ether.

I glanced at the grandfather clock. It was past eight. 'Who the devil would be calling at this hour?' I asked rhetorically.

'Alas, my powers do not extend that far,' Aldo replied.

'Your powers extend no further than luck and inspired guesswork can carry them,' stated Lily, who had never believed in anything that could not be tested under laboratory conditions. She knew, even as she said this, that Aldo was rarely wrong in his predictions, and that at any moment Graves would be letting us know we had a visitor. I had to admire the obstinacy of her scepticism in the face of Aldo's self-evident gifts. But Lily was nothing if not obstinate – and sceptical – about most things.

Aldo once remarked to me that 'many things begin in unexpected places'. He may have been thinking of himself. He was a foundling, you see, discovered in a tea crate on a North London street in the year 1865. One of the nurses at the London Foundling Hospital, where he was subsequently reared, named him Aldo because she thought he looked in some way 'old and Italian'. As for his surname, that came from the location where he was found: Moon Street in Islington. At the age of seven, he was adopted by my father, who desired a companion for me. I was also seven, and somewhat at sea in a house full of adults. I remember my new brother as a thin, grubby boy with poor manners, little education and a general disregard for matters of hygiene and appearance. Yet, even then, he had a quality that marked him out from everyone else I knew. The closest I can come to describing it would be an 'off-centredness', as if his inner compass guided him along alternate paths to those followed by the rest of humanity. Several of Father's acquaintances, who should have known better, voiced their suspicions that he was the son of a witch. Father always laughed off such speculations, saying it was far more likely his parents were something in the tea trade, to judge from the receptacle in which he had been found.

Aldo and I were sent to St Paul's School for Boys, but his strangeness attracted the attention of bullies, and I often felt called upon to rise to his defence. Consequently, I acquired a mostly unmerited reputation for violence. Eventually, Father decided to take us both out of school and hire private tutors to complete our education at home. Now, aged seventeen, Aldo was very much the young gentleman, though, like Lily, he had never entirely managed to shake off his origins. He retained something a little wild in his manner and bearing. He had an animal quickness, combined with an eccentric style of dress. He could charm people, but he could also bemuse and scare them. And he had his powers. As he described it, he had learned to 'feel the ripples in the ether' – enabling him to predict things like knocks on doors.

The knock came.

'Come in, Graves,' I called.

Graves, the butler, entered. He was a tall man, grey and stooped with age after nearly four decades in my family's service. 'The master,' Graves informed us, 'has invited you to join him in the library, where he is entertaining Mrs Rathborn and her son, Mr Daniel Rathborn.'

'Have they just arrived, Graves?'

'Yes, sir,' he bowed.

'By Jove, you were right, Aldo!' I exclaimed. 'What about that then, Lily? Isn't he always right about these things?'

Lily did not comment. She was currently standing before the mirror above the sideboard, checking her appearance. Mr Daniel Rathborn was twenty-five, wealthy and unmarried. He had recently taken over the family legal practice following the death of his father, and must now be considered extremely eligible. Lily would never admit to an interest in him or any other man. She claimed to loathe the very idea of marriage. And yet here she was, straightening her collar and patting down a stray hair. But then Lily was nothing if not contradictory.

My father, Samuel Carter, was a lifelong book lover who had managed to turn his passion to profit with the founding, nearly twenty years ago, of Carter & Jackson Publishers. His partner, Thomas Wilberforce Jackson, retired nine years later, leaving Father as sole proprietor and editor-in-chief. His keen nose for a popular yarn, and clever reissuing of classic tales for younger readers, had reaped him financial rewards, as well as influence in London society. More importantly, as far as Father was concerned, it had helped pay for an extensive collection of first editions of classic adventure novels, now proudly displayed on several of the oak shelves that lined three sides of the library. In the centre of the room, beneath the chandelier, were a pair of Rococo-style sofas on which were seated my father and his guests.

When he saw us enter, Father's eyes twinkled behind the gold-framed spectacles perched on his large, strong nose. 'Come and sit down, you three,' he said. 'You remember the Rathborns, don't you?'

Daniel Rathborn was a tall man with a long, thin nose, high cheekbones and a way of tilting his head back so that he was always looking down on people. I was fairly well acquainted with him, as his father had been, for many years, Carter & Jackson's legal advisor, and Daniel had, in recent times, begun to take over that role. I cannot say I ever much cared for him. Though undoubtedly competent, he had none of his father's jovial, good-natured charm. He affected a kind of graciousness in Father's presence, because he had to, but he had always been rather stiff with me, and scarcely bothered to conceal his dislike of Aldo. I suppose it's possible he feared us – Aldo for his gifts, me for my reputation as a brawler. Or maybe, as I suspected, he was simply not very nice. Tonight, however, he appeared more agitated than rude. He kissed Lily's proffered hand in a perfunctory way with barely a word of greeting, to her obvious disappointment. As I shook his hand, he didn't meet my eye, and looked as though he would rather be anywhere but here.

Mrs Mary Rathborn, by contrast, was always a pleasure. I guessed her to be in her mid-forties, and still a most handsome lady. If her son was a hawk, she was a sparrow, with her petite figure, sharp eyes and quick little movements. Yet this evening, she, too, seemed far from her usual sprightly self. She was wearing the black silk crepe of deep mourning, her husband having passed away less than four weeks earlier, and this emphasised her pallor and the dark smudges of fatigue under her eyes. Naturally, I kept these observations to myself, and merely expressed my delight at seeing the Rathborns.

'Mrs Rathborn wrote to me the other day,' Father explained. 'She mentioned a problem that she and Daniel are experiencing, of a domestic nature–'

'That *she* is experiencing,' interrupted Daniel.

'We happened to be in town this evening,' added Mrs Rathborn quickly. 'We were having dinner with my late husband's executor. And Mr Carter very kindly invited us to come along here afterwards.'

I was gratified that Father had thought to include us in his little evening gathering. It was a sign that we had come of age and were ready to take our places in the world. Gradually, however, as we sat there listening to what the Rathborns had to say, it became apparent that we – or at least one of us – had been called in here for a very particular reason.

CHAPTER

2

espite his scorn for the superstitious rumours surrounding his adopted son, it had not escaped Father's notice that Aldo was a rather special young man. There were many incidents that confirmed him in this view, but three particular episodes stood out. The first took place in the summer of 1873, when Aldo and I were eight, and he was still very much the rough young lad from the Foundling Hospital. We were holidaying with my parents in Lewes, East Sussex. One afternoon, while we were taking a stroll near the castle, Aldo pointed out a small antiquarian bookseller's and told Father that in there he would find *Waverley*. We understood that he meant a first edition of that early

book by Sir Walter Scott, which Father had been seeking for many years. We were amazed that Aldo was even aware of the book and Father's interest in it, and even more astonished to find the novel there under a pile of other books in the rear of the shop. Furthermore, it took Aldo to dig it out – the proprietor had been unaware he had it.

The second occasion took place nearly a year after that. We were returning from a visit to my aunt in Sevenoaks. We had just exited from the train at Charing Cross and were walking through the main station beneath the enormous arched roof of glass and wrought iron, when Aldo stopped and stared up at one of the walls. It looked an ordinary sort of brown-brick wall to the rest of us, and yet fascination, and something like flames, seemed to glitter in Aldo's eyes as he gazed at it. My mother asked him what he was looking at, and Aldo replied 'Fire'. He said: 'The big, long picture is burning'. I looked again at the wall and was confounded if I knew what he was referring to. Only later did we learn that this portion of the station had originally been part of a lecture theatre called Hungerford Hall, which had burned down on 7 April 1854 after a panoramic painting of the Duke of Wellington's funeral had caught fire. Aldo had witnessed the same picture burning twenty years later – to the very day.

The third incident was the most impressive, and affecting. It took place on 21 January 1876, a bitterly cold day that our family will never forget. My mother and Lily's parents were travelling by train on the *Special Scotch Express* to London, returning from a visit to mutual friends in Edinburgh. For business reasons, Father had been called back to London a few days earlier, otherwise he would have been on the train with them. At 6.44 pm, the *Scotch Express*, travelling through heavy snow, reached Abbots Ripton, near Huntingdon, and ploughed straight into a coal train that had failed to observe an earlier stop signal. Aldo and I were at home in the library with Father at the time, freshly bathed and in our pyjamas and dressing gowns, listening to him read us the latest chapter from *Around the World in Eighty Days*. Suddenly, Aldo cried out: 'Mama's dead,' and he burst into tears. The time was 6.44 pm.

We worked out the precise coincidence of timing later, when news of the railway crash reached us and, soon after that, the terrible confirmation that our beloved mother, along with her sister and brother-in-law, were among the fatalities.

As a result of this accident, several things changed in our lives, and ourselves. The most obvious of these was Lily's arrival in our house a few days later. I must confess that although she can be spiteful and capricious, my cousin is never dull. Lily has one of those atmosphere-changing personalities, and her presence certainly helped us get through that first, difficult year without Mother. Almost equally suddenly, Father seemed to grow into an older, frailer, but also unexpectedly warmer person. He shed some of his bookish remoteness and engaged more in our lives, as if doing his best to fill a little of the enormous void that the loss of our mother had left in our family.

I also changed – this I must acknowledge. But the degree of this change has been exaggerated. What people didn't appreciate was that the problems with my temper had always been there. They may have worsened a little after Mother's death, but not as much as has been claimed. If I raised my fists in anger since that time, it was only after intense provocation.

Another, subtler change, and one never really remarked on, was that Father and I began to feel differently about Aldo Moon. We loved him just the same, of course, but that love now also included a strong element of respect, as well as – in my case at least – just a small touch of fear.

But the biggest impact of the accident was felt by Aldo himself. At first he was angry with himself for not foreseeing the train crash, but after much thought he decided that he couldn't be blamed because the universe was essentially a random, chaotic place. Time, he decided, was like a river, flowing from the past to the future. We could guess at what might happen downstream, but we could never know it with certainty. After pondering this a little while longer, he reasoned that if time was a river, there had to be a connection between the present and the future. They were not entirely separate from one another. If a splash were created downstream, such as by the impact of a major future event, it would create ripples, and some of those ripples would flow backwards towards the present. If a sensitive person, such as he, could perceive these ripples, he would be able to predict coming events. He wouldn't be able to say exactly what would happen, only that something would. And the size of the ripple would determine the significance of the event. Of course, he wasn't saying that this river we were floating along was made of water; instead, he called the element we were travelling through the *ether*. This mysterious substance was both spatial and earthly. It surrounded us and connected us to the world, as well as linking us to our past and future. From that time on, Aldo applied himself to the task of perceiving ripples in the ether. It took an effort of will, because our inclination was to focus on what was immediately in front of us. 'We're like rats,' he told me, 'living on a boat that's travelling down this river. And the boat is all we ever see. I can't see outside the boat any more than you can, but I can feel the ripples that rock the boat and I can try and work out what they mean.'

'It began a few weeks ago,' said Mary Rathborn, 'shortly after my husband's funeral. Every night we hear noises coming from downstairs.'

'*You* have heard noises, Mother,' broke in Daniel with some stridency. 'Please don't say *we* when you mean *you*.'

'Daniel claims not to hear them,' said Mrs Rathborn. 'But Mrs Haverhill, our housekeeper, has been disturbed by them, as have two of our maids.'

'The noises will be heard only by those with ears to hear them, Mrs Rathborn,' remarked Aldo.

'Are you accusing me of deafness?' protested Daniel angrily.

'Not at all,' said Aldo. 'You are merely selective about what you choose to hear, as all of us are from time to time. Those parts of life that do not conform to our desires or expectations, we block them out. If I am ever unfortunate enough to find myself at a cricket match, I can assure you, I will not see or hear the playing of a single ball.' He returned his attention to Mrs Rathborn. 'Can you describe the noises, Mrs Rathborn?'

'They vary,' the lady replied. 'Sometimes it's like a deep groaning, as of someone in great pain, and something that might be a stamping of feet or, I don't know, the knocking of a heavy object against floorboards. At other times there is a great crash like furniture being overturned, though we have never found any mess or other signs of disturbance in the morning.'

'Do these sounds come at any particular time in the night?' asked Lily.

'No, my dear,' said Mrs Rathborn, taking a sip of her port. 'They happen at random times. Sometimes they last a few seconds; at other times they endure for several minutes. I can't tell you quite how distressing it is. One starts to fear the prospect of going to bed, knowing that one will be woken at some stage by these dreadful and disturbing sounds.'

'I'm very sorry to hear it, my dear Mrs Rathborn,' said Father warmly. 'You have my deepest sympathies. But do you have any idea what could be causing the sounds?'

'Rats,' said Daniel Rathborn bluntly. 'If there *are* sounds, then they're made by rats.'

'Rats do not groan or stamp their feet,' countered his mother.

I could tell from their expressions that this was a much-visited battleground.

'It is my view,' said Mrs Rathborn in decisive tones, 'that the noises have a spiritual cause.'

'Really, Mother?' sneered Daniel. 'How so?'

'That is what I believe!' declared Mrs Rathborn. 'And that is why we have come here.' For the first time, Mrs Rathborn allowed her gaze to rest fully on Aldo. Lily, seated next to him, was frowning and pursing her lips in an expression of distaste bordering on incredulity.

'You want me to dispose of your little ghost problem,' said Aldo. 'Am I right, Mrs Rathborn?' He spoke sharply, but with a smile.

'In a word, yes.'

'It would be like asking a blind man to find a cat that isn't there,' said Lily, unable to keep quiet any longer. 'I'm sorry, Mrs Rathborn, but it is my firm belief that there are no such things as ghosts or ghostfinders. My cousin may be odd, but he has the same number of senses as the rest of us, which is all he will ever need because nothing exists in this physical world save for what we can see, hear, touch, taste and smell.'

'Bravo,' said Daniel, loudly clapping. She blushed and smiled at this endorsement.

'I admire your conviction, my child,' said Mrs Rathborn. 'But a little humility would do you credit.

As Shakespeare said, "There are more things in heaven and earth, Horatio, than are dreamt of in your philosophy."'

'I have no trouble recognising that my son has certain gifts,' said Father, intervening before an argument could begin. 'And if he feels he can help you, I would not object. My only concern is for him. He has already been the subject of gossip around the town, not all of it kind.'

'Indeed, I remember what happened last summer,' said Mrs Rathborn. 'That must have been a difficult time for you.'

She was referring to the previous July when, for a few weeks, Aldo had become famous as the boy who predicted the shooting of the American President, James Garfield.

Daniel stood up. 'I appreciate what you say, Mr Carter, and your wish to keep quiet about your son's affliction. I firmly believe that if we are to uphold decent Christian values and preserve a society built on reason and common sense, then we must at all costs resist indulging in the type of hysteria and superstition we witnessed last year in the pages of the popular press. I thank you for giving up your time this evening, sir, but I think it best if we now take our leave. And I promise you, Mother, that I will engage the services of a ratcatcher in the morning.'

A smile of approval dawned on Lily's face as she listened to this speech. She seemed delighted to have found an ally in her campaign against the forces of unreason.

Mrs Rathborn, however, was most upset, and refused to rise from her seat, even when Daniel offered his hand to help her up. 'I do not believe that Mr Carter has ever regarded Aldo's gift as an affliction, Daniel,' she pronounced, looking sternly at her son. 'However, I fully understand his desire for privacy.' She then turned to Father. 'We have been friends for many years, Mr Carter. And you know that I have nothing but respect for you and your family. I guarantee that if you were to permit your son to look into this matter for us, we would be the souls of discretion.'

'Mother!' exclaimed Daniel. 'I really think –'

'For our part,' continued Mrs Rathborn, 'we would wish to keep this business strictly between ourselves. One knows how easily word of this sort of thing can spread –'

'And what such absurd and irresponsible talk can do to property prices should we ever feel obliged to sell!' added Daniel.

His mother glared at him, stony-faced. 'You will sell that property over my dead body.'

'Be that as it may,' said Father, breaking the uncomfortable silence. 'I'd like to hear from Aldo.

What do you say, my boy? Do you think you can help?'

'I'm not sure,' said Aldo, looking up from his pocket watch, which he had been gently stroking. 'I have already detected some interesting ripples this evening. I believe your visit here tonight will prove significant in ways that none of us can predict. Whether this means I can help you, I have no idea. But I am eager to try. Of course I will need to spend the night at your house. How soon can I visit?'

Mrs Rathborn clapped her hands in delight on hearing this, and some of her old vigour now returned. 'We would be delighted to have you, Aldo, wouldn't we, Daniel?'

Her son merely glowered.

'In fact,' continued Mrs Rathborn, while casting black looks at Daniel, 'can I suggest that *all* of you come to stay with us for a few days. We have plenty of space at Gravewood Hall, and, heaven knows, the old place could do with some cheering up.'

CHAPTER

3

he following day, after lunch, the Carter family set out for the Rathborn residence in Hertfordshire. We hired two carriages for the journey. Aldo, Lily, myself and Bonnie, Lily's personal maid, travelled in one, and Father, together with James, his valet, and most of the luggage, went in the other.

'Do you suppose Mr Rathborn will be there when we arrive?' asked Bonnie expectantly as we drove along. She was a large, cheerful girl with big green eyes, a round face and rosy complexion.

'Oh, I dare say he'll be at his office in town,' replied Lily with feigned indifference. 'It's Friday, after all.' I could see she had put some work into her appearance this morning. Her bonnet, with its peaked brim, was a little sombre, but her hair had been allowed to fall in ringlets by her ears. She wore a high-necked bodice, but beneath her jacket hem I couldn't help noticing the fashionable *polonaise*-style skirt, with its underskirt showing through.

'He'll be giving us a wide berth these next few days, I should imagine,' I said, a little mischievously.

'And why should you imagine that?' asked Lily, pretending unconcern.

'Because he doesn't want us around,' I replied. 'He wanted to call in the ratcatcher, remember?'

'Oh!' cried Bonnie. 'I don't know which I fear more, rats or ghosts.'

'Mr Rathborn is absolutely right,' said Lily. 'It almost certainly *is* rats. Or the wind. Or the plumbing. He will be most grateful, I am sure, that there is someone among us with plans to investigate this mystery with proper scientific rigour... And why are *you* smiling, Aldo?'

My brother had been gazing out of the carriage window, a grin stretched across his face. 'Because I entirely approve, my dear cousin,' he said, winking at her.

He was a sight to behold, with his hair springing out at every angle from beneath his battered top hat. He wore a shabby velvet coat and violet satin scarf, along with his favourite waistcoat – the red one with the dragon-design front. His restless fingers twirled his silver-topped cane.

'Approve of science?' Lily scoffed. 'I hardly think so. Unless you are claiming that your "ripples in the ether" have some kind of physical basis.'

'I wouldn't care to comment on that,' said Aldo airily. 'Surely what matters is not testability, but results. If my methods prove effective, what does it matter that science cannot explain them?'

'If a quack, by some fluke, cures a patient,' responded Lily, 'you still wouldn't want him to continue practising medicine!'

Aldo laughed. 'Well said, cuz! And maybe you're right. Maybe I *am* a danger to the public.' He frowned and drummed his fingers pensively on the silver ball of his cane. 'I think we ought to use both approaches. If we're going to conduct a thorough investigation, we need to check for physical *and* non-physical causes. I concede that the former, in these types of cases, is always the more likely. Which is why I propose to remain awake tonight. I want all my senses fully alert, including the regular ones.'

'You can count on me for companionship,' I told him.

'Rather you than me, young sirs,' said Bonnie. 'Nights are for sleeping. Nothing I ever wish to see or hear came upon me during the hours of darkness.'

'You never know, Bonnie, your luck may change,' I joked.

'Tut tut, master Nathan,' she giggled. 'You should watch that tongue of yours.'

'But you *must* not sleep tonight,' Lily told Bonnie. 'I need you to keep me company for my own vigil. I have no confidence that these boys can keep their imaginations in check when the noises begin. Only *I* can be trusted to listen and observe dispassionately.'

'Oh, mercy!' said Bonnie, swallowing. 'As you wish, ma'am.'

Gravewood Hall was approached by a winding track between overgrown hedgerows. The front lawn was dominated by a dead, whitish-grey tree with branches silhouetted against the overcast sky like bony, outstretched hands. The house was big, old and ramshackle, with tall, steeply sloping roofs and dark, shuttered windows. Ancient black ivy curled up the sides of the stonework like burnt cobwebs. A flight of cracked steps led to a balustraded terrace and the front entrance.

I could see Lily's face fall as she took all this in. Any flights of fancy she may have entertained about becoming the next Mrs Rathborn were unlikely to have included such a dismal setting.

'Cheerful place, don't you think?' laughed Father, who was waiting for us by the foot of the steps. 'Haunted, do you suppose, Lily?'

'These old places are notorious for their night-time noises, Uncle,' she said stiffly. 'I'm more convinced than ever that there will be a logical explanation for the disturbances.'

The servant who opened the door to us was even older and more stooped than our man, Graves. His welcoming smile revealed several yellow and crooked teeth, and he made a whistling sound as he breathed. I could not help noting the dark splotches on the wallpaper in the gloomy hallway and the general air of damp.

While two young girl servants helped James carry our baggage upstairs, the elderly servant, who introduced himself as Williams the butler, led us into the drawing room. It was a large, cluttered room, full of old furnishings. The stained mirror was crooked, as were the candles in the chandelier, and the rugs, tablecloths and velvet drapery had a faded look.

Mrs Rathborn looked extremely happy to see us, and more like the lively, cheerful woman I remembered from previous meetings – although the dark circles under her eyes were evidence of another interrupted night. 'My friends, how lovely of you to come at such short notice! I hope the journey was not too bad. As you can see, Gravewood Hall remains a work in progress. We inherited it when my father passed away two years ago. It was in a truly dreadful state then, and it feels like we've barely made a mark on it. My dream is to restore it to its former glory, but it is all taking a good deal longer than I supposed it would.'

We conversed for a while about small matters. Aldo said little during these exchanges. He was taking soundings – soaking in the atmosphere of the house through his skin, or so it seemed to me. His eyes were mostly cast downwards towards his watch, which he had removed from his waistcoat pocket and was gently rubbing with his thumb. He often did this when in a sensing mood. Whether the watch held some secret power or was simply an aid to concentration, I couldn't be sure. But it was a beautiful piece, made of silver, with intricate swirling patterns on the case, and gears visible through a viewing window at the front.

The housekeeper, introduced as Mrs Haverhill, brought in tea and a tray of cake. She looked about thirty years of age and had the formidable appearance typical of her kind – with an upright carriage, a long, slightly horsey face, firm, unsmiling mouth and large nose with gently flaring nostrils. Yet there was, perhaps, a hint of weariness in the pinkness of her eyes. Both women looked embattled, as if just living in this place, and trying to bring order and efficiency to it, was a daily struggle, even before the nightly visitations had begun.

At six o'clock, Williams was summoned and Mrs Rathborn asked him to show us to our bedrooms. We followed the old butler as he hobbled up the wide, creaky staircase onto a poorly lit first-floor landing that was so long I could scarcely see to the end of it. The gloom and pervasive smell of damp depressed me. I was shown into a large room at the front of the house. It contained a towering wardrobe, two narrow beds, a washstand, some small tables and an armchair. The deep red flocked wallpaper was peeling above the dado rail, and the net curtains covering the shuttered window were yellow with age. I felt miserable standing there in the cold, uncared-for room, and was already missing my bedroom at home.

I went into Aldo's room, which was next door to mine and similarly furnished, although he had two armchairs.

'What have you picked up so far?' I asked him.

He frowned, perhaps pondering how to translate his vague perceptions into words. 'Unhappiness,' he said at last.

'That could just be me,' I sighed before slumping into one of the armchairs.

Daniel Rathborn arrived at some point after seven o'clock, and joined us for supper. We ate roast venison, followed by apple custard pudding, served up by the stooped, smiling, corpse-like Williams. Although Daniel did not appear at ease in the presence of Aldo and me, he seemed content to be charmed by Lily, who quickly manoeuvred him onto her favourite subject. 'Do you not agree, Mr Rathborn,' she said, 'that we are most fortunate to be alive in this day and age, with men of science such as Darwin, Maxwell and Mendeleev steadily revealing to us the innermost secrets of the universe?'

'Indeed,' said Daniel. 'So far as I can see, the physical universe stands today much like an open book. We understand the mysteries of space and time, of gravity and the motions of the planets and stars. We comprehend the properties of light and sound, the periodicity of the chemical elements and our familial bond with the apes. What more can there be to be discovered?'

'Oh, I do hope there will be more!' declared Lily. 'I plan to dedicate my life to science, and I would be desperately disappointed to find it all understood before I have a chance to embark upon my career.'

'Rest assured, my dear, there is still plenty we do not know,' said Father.

'Like the universe between our ears,' suggested Aldo.

'And what scientific experiment can ever be devised to explain the mystery of love?' said Mrs Rathborn.

'I don't think I wish to understand – or experience – that particular folly,' said Daniel.

'Do you mean that you will never fall in love?' Lily asked him. She had often made similar declarations to Aldo and myself, yet seemed surprised to hear it from another's lips, especially from one whom she had perhaps hoped might one day seek to persuade her of the opposite argument.

'I hope never to, Miss Morelle,' said Daniel. 'Love, from what I have seen, is a very tedious waste of one's energies. It is detrimental to physical and mental health, and distracts one from the pursuit of more wholesome activities.'

Lily smiled at this, and I thought I discerned a new sense of resolution in her brow. I could only guess what it meant, but I suspected she had set herself a challenge with regard to Mr Rathborn.

My father had also seen this look pass across her face, and he said: 'You are very young to speak so cynically, Daniel. I trust when the right woman appears, you will discover a different perspective.'

'My son may be young in years,' sighed Mrs Rathborn, 'but he has the jaundiced views of a much older, more world-weary man.'

At about half past nine, we younger ones retired to our rooms, while Mrs Rathborn, Father and Daniel adjourned to the parlour for a glass of sherry.

Lily and Bonnie bade us goodnight on the landing. Their bedrooms were on the same floor, but located towards the rear of the house. I could see from Lily's stern pout that she was determined, as we were, to confront fearlessly whatever secrets the night held. Bonnie, by contrast, looked shaky with nerves. 'Oh, what a house to find ourselves in. You can be sure of it, ma'am, every creak shall reduce me to raptures of terror. Not a wink shall I sleep tonight.'

'I'm glad to hear it,' said Lily. 'I'm counting on you, Bonnie. Together we shall shine the light of scientific understanding on this mystery.'

Aldo and I decided to carry out our vigil in his room. I used the poker and bellows to revive the fire, while Aldo unpacked the candles he had brought from home and placed them on a small table by the door. Then we made ourselves comfortable in the armchairs. Soon enough the coffees we'd ordered earlier arrived. The maid set the tray down on the bedside table. She looked no more than seventeen. I asked her for her name.

'Alice, sir,' she said. 'Alice Birch.'

'Well, Alice, have you heard anything strange on recent nights?'

'Oh, yes, sir. These past two weeks 'ave been 'orrible. I've 'eard bumps an' groans an' knockin's an' all sorts.'

She was about to take her leave when Aldo suddenly leapt out of his chair and began circling her, his head thrust forward in an almost predatory fashion, his nose sniffing the air around her head as if to catch any whiffs of dishonesty or pretence. 'And what do you suppose is the cause of these sounds?' he barked at her. 'Has the master returned, eh?'

Alice cowered under this onslaught. 'Oh, I don't know, sir,' she quaked. 'It could be the master, I suppose. Or it could be someone up to mischief.'

'And do you know of any potential mischief-makers?'

'None, sir,' she said, flustered. 'Except, now you mention it, there is Polly, sir.'

'Polly?'

'Polly O'Brien, who was the second maid here before Sara. She left about a year ago. Dismissed.'

'Dismissed? Why?'

The girl backed away from Aldo's intense stare. 'I–I'd rather not say, sir, if you don't mind. There were some rumours that I'm sure it wouldn't do for me to repeat. M–may I suggest you speak to Mrs Haverhill as it w–were she who dismissed 'er. S–speakin' of whom sir, and if that will be all, Mrs Haverhill is expectin' me downstairs.'

'Did you need to be so hard on her?' I asked Aldo when Alice had gone.

He handed me a coffee and took a sip from his own. 'Sometimes it helps to stir things up a little,' he said. 'The ripples are felt more clearly. Language, my dear brother... Manners... Etiquette. They're fine for the usual kind of social transaction, but useless for etheric investigation. They so obscure the truth.'

We talked some more about our impressions of Gravewood Hall and its inhabitants, as the embers gradually faded and the house fell quiet, leaving only the sound of the wind whining in the eaves and gently rattling the shutters. At some point, Aldo rose and turned off the pendant oil lamp. Then I must have nodded off because the next thing I knew, my eyes were opening to pitch darkness and I felt a chill in my bones. The wind had eased. Silence lay thickly in the room.

'Did you feel that, Nathan?' came Aldo's deep voice, comfortingly close.

'Feel what?' I asked, and as I said it, I *did* feel something, somewhere on the borderland between sound and touch: a low, juddering growl that was experienced not just in the ears but all over the skin.

'What is it?' I asked.

Aldo was already on his feet, lighting one of the candles. He kneeled and pressed his ear to the floorboards. His gaunt face, thrown into sharp relief by the candle flame, was a study in tense concentration. 'It came from below,' he murmured.

Again I felt it: a tremor in my feet, rising through my legs, my chest, my head. It nagged like an old beggar, like a needy child. A picture of that dead tree came to me, with its branches like upturned hands. It wasn't a sound but an emotion – a kind of desperate pleading. And Aldo was right: it was coming from beneath us.

'I must go downstairs,' he announced when the thing had stopped. And then, quite suddenly, he was gone, out of the door, taking the candle with him.

I rose, planning to follow him, but collided with his chair in the darkness. With fumbling hands

I managed to light another candle and get myself out onto the landing, but by then Aldo was nowhere to be seen.

The stairs creaked awfully, and I felt sorry for the others in their beds listening fearfully to the sound of my footsteps. Yet I was sorrier still for myself for having to descend alone into the black spaces below, and irritated with Aldo for not waiting for me.

I reached the foot of the stairs, still with no idea of where he was. I felt very alone, and the melancholy moonlight from the leaded window above the front door only deepened my sense of isolation. Beyond that, and the modest reach of my candle, all was shadow.

The dark began to play tricks with my eyes. A tall clock seemed to lean in towards me like a malevolent stranger. A hallway chair, glimpsed in dimmest outline, had a figure seated in it – until I saw this was just a pattern carved into its high back. As I stood there, trying not to see the things the darkness wished to divulge, I began to feel a tightening of the skin. There was something further up the hallway, I was sure of it. And it was coming slowly towards me. All was thick shadow, but I sensed it creeping along the hall floor, getting closer. I couldn't move for terror. It came as a whispery trembling on the air, a pleading sorrow that was not quite sound, almost like a papery touch on the skin. The darkness itself seemed to breathe. It was unbearable.

Crash! Like a heavy coffin falling on a stone floor, the noise was so sudden and loud that I dropped my candle and was cast into terrifying blackness. I heard a whimper of fear in my throat. This was as real as physical assault. It was huge, whatever it was, and coming for me. A glow in the darkness, like a demon's eye, was flickering towards where I stood. I had already turned to flee back up the stairs when I heard a shout.

'Nathan!'

The demon's eye was the flame of Aldo's candle.

'Follow me!' he yelled and he chased off down the hall. I forced my legs to move, to follow him, even though I was sure, still, there was something there, waiting for us. His candle illuminated the blotchy walls, the grimy oil paintings, a door leading into another room. I saw him look through the door and felt certain he would see it then. But he didn't recoil. His lips only parted in mild surprise, then he dashed into the room and I was left in darkness.

'Nathan! Come and look!'

I followed him into the room. It was a library – high-ceilinged, but not big – containing nothing more monstrous than books. There were three tall sash windows opposite the doorway. Two were closed and shuttered, but the shutters of the right-hand one were thrown wide open, as was the lower sash, admitting an icy draft into the room, and a thick, stone-coloured beam of moonlight across the wooden floor. In the centre of the room a large oak library table lay on its side. Numerous books, which must until recently have covered the surface of the table, were spilled about the floor. The other sides of the room were completely lined with shelves containing row upon row of dusty old tomes, reaching high up into the shadowy recesses near the ceiling.

Aldo was at the window peering out. He couldn't have seen anything there, for he returned to the middle of the room and examined the overturned table. By this time, footsteps could be heard on the stairs, and soon we were joined by most of the household, including Lily, Bonnie, Father, Mrs Rathborn, Mrs Haverhill, Alice, Sara and Father's valet James.

'A poltergeist!' swooned Bonnie when she saw the mess in the room.

'Did you see anything, boys?' asked Father.

'No, Father,' said Aldo, replying for me, for I was still trying to get my breathing under control. 'But at least we know it wasn't a ghost,' he added, pointing to the open window. 'Someone is playing a trick on you, Mrs Rathborn, and whoever it was escaped through that window.'

'We've never seen a mess like this before,' whispered a shocked-sounding Mrs Rathborn.

'The intruder heard Nathan and me coming,' said Aldo, 'so had to make a quick escape. Otherwise he or she might have stayed to tidy up.'

'Can we go after them?' asked Mrs Rathborn.

'Whoever it was, they'll be far away by now,' said Father. 'We can inform the police about this in the morning.'

Lily, despite being dressed in only a thin nightgown, had gone over to the cold of the open window and was studying the frame. 'This wasn't a break-in,' she announced. 'This window was unbolted from the inside.'

Mrs Haverhill turned to Alice. 'Did you bolt the library windows tonight, Alice?' she asked.

'Yes, missus,' cried Alice. 'Shut and bolted, like every night.'

'Well, clearly that one wasn't,' said Mrs Haverhill sharply. 'Or else how do you suppose the intruder got in?'

'I'm sure I don't know, missus,' said Alice, close to tears.

'Well close it now, girl,' ordered Mrs Haverhill. 'And then get yourself to bed.'

The gathering at the library doorway soon broke up as we returned to our rooms. I was feeling very sleepy by this time and, by common consent, the vigil was at an end.

Before we parted for the night, I stopped Aldo on the landing outside his room. 'There was something else though, wasn't there?' I said. 'We both felt it while we were up here, and it was even stronger downstairs.'

'Oh yes,' he said enthusiastically, his eyes glinting in the halflight. 'There most certainly was!'

'What did you sense?'

'Someone,' he said in a low voice. 'There is a spirit in this house, and it's desperately unhappy. Something happened here – something tragic. But promise me, brother, that you won't say anything to the others, at least not yet.'

'But there was physical evidence,' I said. 'The mess in the library, the open window. Everyone saw that.'

'That's true,' he nodded. 'And as far as the rest of them are concerned, it points to nothing more than a simple break-in. Well, let's not disagree. You don't have to have etheric sensibilities to see that Daniel doesn't like us being here. Maybe the man has something to hide, I don't know. But he will probably do everything he can to discredit us. In which case it would not do to reveal our hand too early. Timing is all, my dear Nathan. Timing is all! We shouldn't reveal what we know until we have evidence to back it up.'

'But we both heard that sound, Aldo. That was evidence, wasn't it?'

'I'm not sure we *heard* anything,' he smiled. 'We both *felt* something, and, you know…' – he gave a faint chuckle – 'I think there may just be a touch of the sensitive in you too, brother. The trouble is I've taken so much abuse over the years for this so-called gift. People want my help, but they don't like me for it, and they don't want to believe in it either. That's why I always seek other evidence to give credence to these… feelings. These ripples I pick up aren't subject to rational analysis. They can't be felt or measured by any machine, so it's easy for the likes of Daniel and Lily to dismiss it all. Which is why perception is key, Nathan. Above all, if we're going to crack this case, we have to use our eyes and ears, as well as any other powers we can call upon.'

CHAPTER

4

'I don't believe there is any need to send for the police,' said Daniel Rathborn the following morning. 'After all, nothing was stolen. It was probably just children from the village.' We were in the morning room eating a breakfast of kippers and poached eggs. Outside, it was cold and bright. The sun shone dustily through the window pane, glinting on the plates and silverware. With the bustle of servants and the crackle and pop of fresh logs on the fire, the place seemed almost homely, and the fears of the night now struck me as faintly absurd.

'Whether or not you wish to involve the police is your choice,' said Father, putting down his fork. 'But it is surely time you faced the facts, Daniel.

Last night was merely the latest in a series of nocturnal disturbances. In my view, village children would not be capable of such a sustained campaign. This whole thing smacks of something planned and premeditated. If the intruder's motive isn't theft, then why is he doing it? I suspect his desire is to scare the occupants of this house and make your lives here a misery. And in Mrs Rathborn's case, at least, he is succeeding. You must start to wonder if there is anyone in the local community, or beyond, who wishes you ill. If you don't want this to be a police matter, then you will need to do some investigating yourself. Or else leave it to my boys and my niece, who I'm sure will be only too happy to help.'

Mrs Rathborn placed a supportive hand on Father's arm and smiled warmly at him, encouraged by his robust and commonsense challenge to her son.

'I cannot imagine who would bear a grudge against this family, Mr Carter,' said Daniel tetchily. 'Mother and I are quiet, law-abiding people. We go to church every Sunday, pay our taxes. We do our duty as members of the local community. We have no enemies here. But neither are we entirely accepted yet, being relative newcomers to Winterby. And the last thing we want is to have your family conducting an enquiry, alarming the staff and the people of the village with their questions and accusations. And count on it, what is heard in the servants' hall at lunchtime is common knowledge at the Old Cock Inn by sundown.'

'No one is planning to make accusations, Mr Rathborn,' said Aldo. 'We want to find out the truth, that is all, and we will invite the servants to help us search for it.'

Daniel looked down his narrow, suspicious nose at Aldo.

'Dear Mr Rathborn,' said Lily sweetly. 'We will be the souls of discretion, I assure you. You have my personal promise that I will keep my cousins in line.'

He looked at her a moment, seemingly struck by her charming smile and earnest tone. He gave a small bow. '*You* I am prepared to trust, Miss Morelle.'

Mrs Rathborn, Daniel and Father had arranged to call upon mutual friends in Bishop's Stortford that day, promising to return by evening. Before their departure, Mrs Rathborn gave us the use of a back room for the purpose of conducting interviews. The light here was fairly poor, but the room was cosy, with a Persian rug and generously stuffed armchairs. I hoped the relaxed informality would be conducive to truthfulness.

Our first interviewee was Mrs Haverhill. She eyed Lily, Aldo and me suspiciously as she came in. 'I hope this won't take up too much time,' she said. 'I have the household accounts to do this morning, and then have to check the linen, and place orders for flour and spices and whatever else Cook will ask me for.'

'Have no fear, Mrs Haverhill,' said Lily. 'We shall not keep you longer than is strictly necessary.'

Mrs Haverhill sat with her back ruler-straight on the edge of the armchair. Clearly she didn't approve of comfortable furniture and would not allow herself to be seduced by its vulgar charms.

'Do you have any theories about what might be causing these disturbances?' asked Lily.

'Oh, we can all theorise, Miss, but I don't know what you expect to achieve by it. Why, it could be bats or foxes for all I know. Or it could be the master come back to haunt us. There's no telling what it might be.'

'Yes, well, that's true,' I said placatingly, for I could see she was both impatient and ill at ease. 'We just thought, as you have been living with this... phenomenon... a little longer than us, you might have formed some ideas about it. For example, you mentioned just now that it might be the ghost of John Rathborn. Do you have any reason to think that?'

'None at all!' she cried. 'Why should you think so? I just mentioned it among a list of things, including bats and foxes.

'Yes, but it seems an odd thing to mention, unless you had some reason–'

'I don't see why you should think it odd. The master died not a month ago, and isn't it often the way that people put such things down to the ghosts or spirits of the lately departed?'

'So there's nothing that led you to suggest that,' I persisted, 'except the fact that he recently passed away?'

'I haven't *seen* him since he went into the earth, if that's what you mean.'

'Can we move on?' said Lily, flashing me one of her sharp looks. She smiled at the housekeeper. 'I so agree with you, Mrs Haverhill, that theorising about what might be causing the disturbances is not a helpful line of enquiry, and I am sorry I ever embarked on it. Let us focus instead on the facts of the case. Can I ask you, Mrs Haverhill, to describe what you *have* witnessed, that is, what you have seen or heard, during recent nights.'

'Bumps mostly,' answered Mrs Haverhill. 'As well as creaks, taps and scratchings.'

'Anything else?'

'Crashes. Like the one we heard last night.'

'Mrs Rathborn mentioned hearing a groaning sound,' I said.

'Yes, well, I never heard anything like that,' said Mrs Haverhill. Then she rose to her feet. 'If that is all,' she said, 'then I really must be getting on with my work. This household doesn't run itself, you know.'

'Just one moment, Mrs Haverhill,' called Aldo, leaping to his feet. Until that point he'd been lounging on an armchair near the back of the room, one foot propped on a small table, gently stroking his pocket watch, seemingly oblivious to the world around him.

Mrs Haverhill glanced at him impatiently. 'Yes? What is it, young sir?'

Aldo strode to within a few feet of her. Head thrust forward, hands behind his back, he peered closely at the housekeeper. I prayed he would employ a gentler approach than he had with poor Alice Birch.

'Why did you dismiss Polly O'Brien?' he barked at her.

The housekeeper looked shocked. 'How did you know about that?' she spluttered.

Aldo stepped back, looking pleased with himself, while Lily looked on in reluctant admiration. This was a masterly surprise attack from a completely unexpected direction.

'It was Alice, wasn't it?' Mrs Haverhill raised her eyes heavenwards. 'When will that girl ever learn to guard her tongue?'

'And what is your answer, my good woman?' urged Aldo.

'I'm sure I don't know what this has to do with anything.'

'Please answer the question,' I said.

The housekeeper sighed and retook her seat. 'She got herself pregnant, if you must know. It was almost exactly a year ago. Of course, she had to go. But I was pleased, if I'm to be honest, for the excuse to be shot of her. She was never much good as a maid. Her work was shoddy, she talked too much, was untidy in her habits, and was frequently late for duty.'

'What became of her?' asked Lily.

'I believe she remained in Winterby village a while, living with a local bricklayer named Culpin. Richard Culpin. He's still living here, in the village. But Polly left him shortly after the birth of her child. I don't know where she went. Possibly to her sister in London. I've not seen nor heard from her since.'

'Did she bear a grudge against you or the Rathborns?' asked Aldo.

'A grudge? I don't think so. She could hardly blame *us* now, could she? What choice did we have?'

After Mrs Haverhill, we interviewed the maid Sara Teltree, a pale waif of about fifteen, with a melancholy face and a pronounced limp, which, she explained, was due to her left leg being an inch too short. With a clumsy attempt at humour, I ventured that it might be her right leg that was, in fact, an inch too long. The girl only stared sadly at me, and Lily shot me another of her dagger-like glances. Sara could tell us little that we didn't already know about the nocturnal sounds, or anything else for that matter. She had worked at the house for less than twelve months, she told us, and was not a local from the village, like Alice, having been recruited by the mistress from the reform school in Hertford. Being in Sara Teltree's doleful company for even a quarter of an hour quite deflated my spirits – and for no apparent gain, although I was surprised to overhear Aldo muttering to himself, after she had left: 'That girl knows a great deal more than she is saying.'

Thus far in our investigations, the only person we had uncovered with a possible motive for the nightly intrusions was Polly O'Brien – assuming she hadn't gone off to London – and we agreed that this angle was worth pursuing further. After lunch, we invited the other maid, Alice Birch, to come into the back parlour, and asked her for her recollections of Polly.

'A cheerful girl, she was, with beautiful flame-red hair,' recalled Alice, her eyes soft with nostalgic memories. 'Worldly, you might call 'er, maybe a touch proud, but always so amusin'. I loved to 'ear 'er stories about the people she'd worked for in London, and the things she'd seen. But she was forever in trouble with Mrs Haverhill. Weren't very good at the basic stuff, see, like keepin' her uniform clean and wakin' up on time. An' she found it 'ard to keep 'er opinions to 'erself when talkin' to Mrs Haverhill or the mistress. Though the master 'ad a soft spot for 'er, I could tell. She 'ad this kind of confidence, as if she were born for better things than bein' a maid. She used to dream of marryin' someone with money, so she could live the 'igh life. All dreams o' course.'

'Did you keep in touch with her after her dismissal?' I asked.

'I saw 'er on me Sunday afternoons off, after she'd taken up with Culpin, the bricklayer. She said 'e would take care of 'er, though most of the time I saw 'im 'e was drunk.'

'Why did she leave him, do you think?'

'Dunno. Maybe 'e beat 'er. She was too good for 'im anyways. I always like to think she met a better man, or else she made a new start in London, maybe on the stage. She was never goin' to settle for this sort of life.' Her face grew sad. 'But then on other days, I see 'er lyin' dead, 'er and 'er little Jimmy, in some city backstreet. With a girl like that, always takin' 'er chances, never thinkin' 'bout the consequences, a bad end was always just as likely.'

'I'm surprised,' mused Lily, 'that this Culpin fellow didn't try to find her, considering that she'd taken off with his son.'

Aldo emitted a sudden bark of laughter, making Alice jump with fright. 'Aha!' he cried. 'But Richard Culpin wasn't Jimmy's father, was he?' Lily and I looked at him, startled to find our lackadaisical colleague once more apparently ahead of the game.

'Well, there was a rumour,' murmured Alice, 'but I'm sure it wouldn't do for me to repeat it.'

'Yes, that's exactly what you said last night,' Aldo chuckled. 'And now I know what you mean by it. You gave us a clue earlier when you said the master had a soft spot for her. Jimmy's father was John Rathborn, am I right?'

Alice flushed and looked down. 'That was the rumour, yes sir.'

Alice was resolutely vague about where this information had come from. She called it a village rumour, but refused to say explicitly from where in the village it had originated. She urged us not to tell anyone else, especially not her mistress, 'as it would surely break 'er heart'.

After Alice had left, we three sat around and discussed what, if anything, we should do with this information, which might, in the end, prove nothing more than a piece of malicious and ill-founded gossip. It certainly took us no further along in terms of the case. Of course, it was possible that Polly O'Brien had had an affair with John Rathborn and that, after discovering her condition, he had ended the relationship and perhaps even asked Mrs Haverhill to dismiss her. This might conceivably have led the woman to wage a campaign of vengeance against the person who had rejected her. But the cheerful, happy-go-lucky Polly O'Brien, as described by her friend Alice Birch, did not seem this type of woman. And even if she had been, why wait a whole year, by which time the target of her fury was dead?

Our final interviewee of the day was Mrs Partridge, the cook. She was a stout, good-natured lady of perhaps forty, with a large chin and dimpled cheeks. She was inclined to wander into conversational tangents, and it took an effort to keep her to the subject at hand.

'Oh, don't ask me about the nights,' she said. 'I sleep like a log, always have, ever since I was a girl. But I've most certainly heard noises during the day, and I'm not talking about the usual kind of bang and clatter you'd hear in a busy kitchen. I'm talking about knockings and rustlings. I thought at first it might be rats. Nasty, horrible things. I've seen them on occasion and they terrify me. Some as large as puppies, and they don't scare easy – just sit and stare at you as if *you're* the intruder. We used poison to get rid of them.'

'About those noises, Mrs Partridge?'

'Ah yes, well then I thought it might be cock-a-roaches. I've a special fear of cock-a-roaches, being as they like kitchens and darkness, and they always come in swarms. Nancy, our scullery maid, is even more scared than I. She must get up early to light the oven, and she's often seen them scurrying into corners when she turns the light on.

'Do you think the noises are made by cockroaches, then?'

'Oh, I don't think so. They're too loud to be caused by any insect. I don't know what causes them, but more than once I've mistaken them for someone knocking at the kitchen door.' This must have triggered a memory, for she suddenly burst into laughter. 'And then there was the time I mistook a real knock at the door for the noises. The 15th of October, it was – my birthday. I got such a fright when the door suddenly opened – I had imagined it might be a ghost, but it was only Alice,

Sara and Mr Williams come to wish me many happy returns. Mrs Haverhill couldn't be there as she was on a shopping expedition in Hertford. But the mistress was there. I was so touched. She said to me: "Take the night off, Mrs P. We're going out to a restaurant in Hertford." "But the chicken stew is ready," I told her, pointing at the pan on the hob. "It only wants serving." She went over and tasted it and told me it was perfect, and would keep till tomorrow. So I was to have the night off, put my feet up, or so I thought. But then an apologetic note came down a little later to say that only the mistress and Mr Daniel were going out. The master was staying in. He had objected to the plan, being as he hadn't been consulted and he always hated going out anyway.'

At that point, we thanked Mrs Partridge for her time and terminated the interview.

During supper that evening, Mrs Rathborn and Father questioned Aldo and me about our progress. We confessed that we had made very little, but told them of our plans to go to Winterby village the following day to see what we might discover there. I was distracted from saying much more in response to their questions, thanks to Lily, who had opted to dress quite uncharacteristically that evening. She wore a pale pink, sleeveless, low-necked dress with a tight bodice and a full skirt – I had rarely seen so much of her on display. She and Daniel were engaged in intimate conversation, of which I only caught snatches. He was telling her about their day in Bishop's Stortford, and she was listening and nodding, but saying little. When she *did* speak, the tone of her voice seemed warmer and gentler than usual. I noticed she frequently widened her eyes and emitted little gasps of surprise and amusement at the things he was saying. Her hair was swept up to the top of her head and some of it was frizzled over her forehead, so she often needed to brush a strand delicately from her eye as she gazed up at him.

Daniel Rathborn struck me as a very dubious object for all this effort. The man was brusque to the point of rudeness – at least in his dealings with Aldo and me – and he had already made plain his antagonism to the very notion of love. That said, he was evidently enjoying the attention she was presently lavishing on him, and was more expansive, relaxed and pink-cheeked than I'd seen him before.

Watching them huddled in their affectionate twosome at the far end of the table, I resolved never again to listen to people who speak of rejecting love as a matter of principle. They are, all of them, liars and hypocrites.

So bemused was I by the love birds that I almost failed to catch Aldo's surprise announcement, towards the end of the meal, that he planned to spend the night in the library. As I heard these words, I swiftly turned back to Father and Mrs Rathborn and impulsively declared that I would join him there. Mrs Rathborn asked us repeatedly whether we were really sure we wanted to do this, but Aldo was resolute that this was the only way of discovering the identity of the intruder. By this time, recalling the terror I had experienced the night before, I began to wonder whether I had perhaps been a little hasty in my decision, and if there was some way of gracefully backing out of it. I decided, regretfully, that there wasn't, and Mrs Rathborn started to instruct the servants to set up twin beds in the library and light the fire. But Aldo informed her that none of this would be necessary, indeed it would be counterproductive.

'The room must be left exactly as it was last night,' he insisted. 'We do not wish the intruder to know we are there: we want to observe him or her, if possible, in the act!'

'But it will be very cold and uncomfortable for you,' Mrs Rathborn fretted.

'We can wear our coats,' said Aldo. 'And the library armchairs will be perfectly comfortable, am I right, Nathan?'

'Indeed,' I muttered.

'But this could be most dangerous, don't you think, Mr Carter?' said Mrs Rathborn. 'We have no idea what sort of character this intruder is. Are you happy for your sons to expose themselves to danger in this way?'

'Anyone who's witnessed Nathan in a scrap will know he's perfectly capable of taking care of himself,' answered Father, smiling at me. 'As for Aldo, I'm sure he'll be able to sense the intruder long before he can get close to them.'

'Well at least let me provide each of you with a revolver,' said Mrs Rathborn.

'I hardly think that's necessary, Mother,' objected Daniel, who had paused in his duologue with Lily for long enough to overhear this.

But Mrs Rathborn would not be overruled, and after supper, Williams provided each of us with a fully loaded double-action revolver from a secret cache in his basement office.

'These were Mr John's,' wheezed the old butler, with a smile displaying the full glory of his deplorable dentalwork. 'Very keen on security, he was, though he never got the chance to use them on a trespasser, not a human one at any rate.'

Aldo was presented with a Lefaucheux 12 millimetre, while I was favoured with the more modern, and British, Tranter .44. The weight of the weapon in my hand provided an immediate boost to my confidence.

'I wish tonight most fervently that I wasn't a girl, and I could join you boys in your adventuring,' said Lily, before departing for her room. As I had learned tonight, there could be a formidable gap between what Lily said and what Lily did, but I could see this time that she was speaking the truth. My cousin may have been a hypocrite in matters of love, but she had pluck – more, certainly, than I had. Of course, she did have the impervious carapace of her scientific faith to protect her, while my primitive mind lay naked and exposed to all manner of dark and unnatural fears.

'Come now, my lady,' said Bonnie. 'It is surely a man's great misfortune that he should feel compelled by virtue of his sex to face danger for its own sake. I for one would not swap places with either of them for all the tea in China.'

Dressed in our outer coats and armed with revolvers and candles, Aldo and I made our way along the hallway to the library. The fear that had seized me the previous night was no longer there, but I still felt uneasy entering the room. In the light of the pendant oil lamp, we saw that the large rectangular table, which dominated the centre of the room, had been restored to its upright position with the books replaced on its surface, and all three windows were shut and bolted. In every other respect the room was exactly as we had found it the night before. Unlike the morning room on the far side of the hall, the library had no access to the back garden, just a wall of books where the other room boasted a set of French windows. The southern and western walls of the room were also dense with shiny, well-worn book spines, a vast array broken only by the fireplace and chimney breast, and the door by which we had entered.

I moved to the east wall and unbolted and opened the central sash window, then raised the latch and threw open the shutters. A bracing blast of wintry air swirled around me. The moon, glowing silkily through thick, fast-moving clouds, illuminated the tiny flakes of snow that gusted down onto frost-stiffened grass and pools of gleaming black ice in the heavily rutted track. Just beyond was a dense wood of tall trees, their bony, trembling branches leaning in towards the roof of the house. The wood's scale and closeness felt oppressive, and the specks of snow were blowing into my face, so I quickly reclosed the window. Even on the sunniest days, I imagined the library would be a gloomy place – good for the preservation of books, no doubt, but not welcoming to people. It didn't surprise me that, according to Williams, the room was scarcely used, 'except by Mr John, sir, who had an aversion to bright sunlight ever since he was a boy'.

Aldo extinguished the light, and we felt our way towards two of the armchairs positioned at the northern end of the room, where we settled down to wait.

'Well, Nathan,' he said in his deep voice. 'Are you ready for what the night will bring?'

'I'm not sure I am,' I said.

'No, nor I.'

The previous night I had missed the comfort of home and bed, but at least we'd had the warmth and light of a fire for solace. Tonight the darkness was complete – I could not see my hand before my face – leaving me exposed to whatever fearful shapes my imagination chose to conjure. And even though I raised my collar and drew my coat close around me, the November chill found a way of seeping into my bones.

Slowly, my eyes adapted to the dark and I was able to perceive in dim outline the table with its piles of books, the other chairs and, very obscurely, the jut of the chimney breast on the far side of the room. To my left, I could make out some of Aldo's profile. His head and body were back as far as they could sink between the wings of his armchair. I could not tell if his eyes were open or closed.

Like this we waited, for an hour, maybe two, and gradually, over that long, deep, wakeful silence, a vague feeling of unease stole over me. There was something quite repugnant about this room, I decided. It wasn't the chill, nor the closeness of the overbearing trees outside, nor the incident last night, nor even what might happen again tonight, but something else. I had been aware of it from the moment I'd entered – it was probably why I had opened the window – yet it was only now that I felt able to admit it to myself. I don't like the word *evil* – it is so overused – yet it was the only word that seemed to suit the atmosphere in this room. Evil had been done here, and the evil, somehow, remained. With an urgency that bordered on panic, I was suddenly seized by a compulsion to leave the room, the house, even.

But then a calmer part of me tried to assert itself. I recalled Aldo's words: be wary of imagination; perception was the key. What were my senses actually telling me? Look, I said to myself, the shapes in the room have not shifted a quarter of an inch in all my time of staring at them. And no sound has reached my ears these past few hours, save for the soft, echoey tick of the clock in the hall. The odour of mildew, which clings like old lakeweed to every part of this house, is no stronger now than before. But, that other part of me insisted, there *is* something else here, in this room, beyond sight, beyond sound, beyond smell. It presses on my heart, constricts my breath, prickles my skin in dreadful anticipation of its touch.

And then... it stirred. It actually...

Something was moving in the blackness to my right. At the very extremity of my vision, I saw it: a shifting in the shadows. I froze, not even daring to turn my head. My hand groped for the gun, but it caught on a fold and I was too weak to pull it from my pocket. I could only sit there, rigid, my muscles brittle like ice, my stomach melting. For, you see, the thing was *breathing*! I could hear it in the darkness, very close – loud, agitated breathing, as you might hear in Bedlam late at night. And then there came a soft moan, so close I could almost feel it disturb the air next to my cheek. Infinitely deep and sad it was, like a dog trapped by its neck on cold ground – the most harrowing sound I ever heard. It bled right down into my bones. I prayed for it to stop, prayed I would never live to hear it again.

Silence finally returned, save for the tick of the clock and the battering ram of my heart.

'Aldo!' I managed to sob. 'Aldo!'

'It's alright,' he whispered. 'I think it's gone.'

'What was it?'

Before he could reply, the door was suddenly flung open and something huge and grey flew in from the hall. I started up from my chair but then my vision began to swim and everything melted away to nothing.

When I awoke it was to a squall of cold air on my face and the sight of snowflakes blowing in through the open window. Aldo was sprawled face down on the floor. The library table was, once more, on its side, with books spilled everywhere. By the time I had rallied myself sufficiently to light a candle, people were already arriving in the room. Most of the household had once again gathered, though not the master. Lily and my father immediately ran to Aldo, while Mrs Haverhill went to close the window.

Aldo had a cut on his forehead, but was conscious. 'I'm fine,' he insisted, but Mrs Haverhill sent Sara for a clean, damp towel.

'Did you catch him?' Aldo asked.

'Catch whom?' queried Father.

Aldo banged a frustrated fist on the floor. He turned to me with feverish urgency. 'Nathan, did you get a look at the man?'

'Was it a man?' I stammered. 'Are you sure?'

'What else then?' he asked furiously.

'I saw something big and grey,' I said. 'It could have been anything. It happened so fast, I–'

'What did *you* see, Aldo?' asked Mrs Rathborn.

'A man,' he said, wincing as Lily pressed the towel to his forehead. 'I'm certain it was a man. He came into the room from the hall. He wore a bulky grey cloak, with a bag or something over his face. I tried to confront him, but he rushed up and clouted me. That's all I remember.'

'That was very brave of you, Aldo,' said Mrs Rathborn. 'I'm so sorry you were hurt.'

'How strange that you weren't able to predict his arrival in your usual fashion,' Lily smiled mischievously.

Aldo looked at her with mild irritation. 'I was distracted by something else,' he said simply.

'And what was that?'

Aldo merely shook his head.

'So we've learned a little more tonight,' concluded Father. 'The intruder is a man... probably! And he's gaining access to the house by some other means than the library. Alice, your conscience is clear!'

'Thank-you kindly, sir,' came Alice's voice from near the door.

'What's more, a pattern seems to be emerging. The invasion took place just after midnight, as it did yesterday. It seems our trespasser is a creature of regular habits. Now all we must do is find out how he's getting in, and…' Father trailed off, frowning at me. 'Nathan, are you alright? You look dreadful.'

'I–I'm fine,' I coughed.

Lily was also studying me. 'Is there anything else, Nathan? Any clues that could help us?'

'No,' I said shakily. 'I just want to go to bed.'

CHAPTER

5

he snow piled up in huge drifts during the night, effectively cutting us off from the world. There would be no going to church this Sunday morning, nor any expedition to the village to further our investigations. I could not say I was sorry about this, as I was in a poor state, both physically and mentally. In fact, I remained in bed until noon, feeling not exactly ill, but curiously weak and distracted. At some point during the morning, Williams hobbled in with a pile of books from the library, 'courtesy of the mistress', but I was unable to concentrate on any of them for more than a few paragraphs, for my thoughts constantly wandered back to the previous night.

The big grey figure seemed less troubling to me in the cold light of day. He was, undoubtedly, a man, as Aldo had claimed. He'd had substance, as evidenced by the blow to Aldo's head, and his odd, baglike shape was due, surely, to his outfit and the poor light. No, what really disturbed me was the recollection of what had happened just before the intruder's entrance.

The memory of that frantic breathing, so close to my cheek, and that desolate moan – the lament of a soul in extreme torment – was enough to cleave me to my bed that morning. Heaven knows I tried to distract my mind with other things but, try as I might, I could not purge my ear of those sounds, which I heard again and again as clearly as if I were still seated in that darkened room downstairs. And each time I heard them, my limbs would turn to jelly, my innards to ice, and sweat would break forth from my hot skin until the sheets were quite soaked with it.

Finally, the smells of luncheon and the hustle and bustle of servants coaxed me from my bed. I washed my face in a bowl of tepid water, brought earlier to my chamber by Sara, and slowly dressed. My room was at the front of the house, and I could see from my window that the lawn and the winding track between the hedgerows were covered in a thick layer of snow, great flakes of which were still falling. It was a cheering sight. Even the big, dead tree in the middle of the lawn looked a little less bleak now that its beseeching, claw-like branches were gloved in large dollops of snow. The wood to the east of the house – the same one that was visible from the library – was also less ominous today, and far more picturesque in its snowy mantle. How startling was the transformative effect on the human spirit of a little crystalline water ice – as Lily would doubtless say!

As I observed the wood, my eye was caught by a movement to the south. I turned in time to see a figure – it looked like a woman in a dark cloak – disappearing round a bend of the twisting track that led to the main road. How strange that I hadn't seen her cross the lawn just now. I assumed it was Mrs Haverhill or one of the maids off to the village on their afternoon off. But what a day to attempt such a journey!

Then, with a start, I noticed another odd thing: there were no footprints in the snow-covered lawn or track to mark the woman's progress from the house. Where had she come from if not from there? The figure had been visible for just a second or two, but I had seen her! Was there perhaps some other property beyond the hedgerow that I was unaware of? I was still puzzling over this mystery when I heard the gong announcing lunch.

The entire household was gathered in the dining room when I arrived. I was very hungry, having missed breakfast, and eagerly tucked into my bowl of beef stew and potatoes. Daniel reported that the roads were currently impassable, even on horseback, so there was no possibility of getting a message to the police. 'We've checked and double-checked every door and window to this property,' he said, 'and they were all locked last night, so his means of access remains a mystery. At least this intruder, whoever he may be, does not seem intent on anything but making a noise. Unless provoked, that is,' he added with a disapproving nod at Aldo, who was sporting a small bandage around his head.

I asked Daniel if any of the servants had left the house during the past hour.

'Only Williams,' he replied, 'to fetch more wood from the shed. And Johnson, the groom, may have gone to the stable.'

'No women then?'

Daniel shook his head. 'Why do you ask?'

'I saw a woman heading out along the track towards the village not a quarter of an hour ago.'

'I'm sure you didn't,' Daniel snapped. 'It was probably a deer.'

'I'm so glad to hear you have rediscovered your powers of observation this morning, Nathan,' laughed Lily, 'even if it *is* to mistake a deer for a woman. That is certainly an improvement on last night when you fainted before managing to see anything at all.' She exchanged amused glances with Daniel.

Feeling the familiar heat rising beneath my collar, I shouted across the table: 'Go to the devil, cousin! And as for you, sir!' I yelled at Daniel, who was still grinning. 'I have not heard *you* volunteering to spend the night in a cold, dark room waiting for a dangerous trespasser to appear. It would serve you well to remember we are doing all this as a favour to *you*.'

'Not to me,' said Daniel quietly. 'I did not ask you to come here.'

'Daniel!' said Mrs Rathborn angrily. 'Remember who you are speaking to. I'm so sorry, Mr Carter. You are our honoured guests and, of course, extremely welcome. Please don't take offence.'

'None taken,' said Father, who then cast a stern look at me. 'Nathan, that was rude, and the language was ungentlemanly. Please apologise to Lily and Mr Rathborn immediately.'

I stared at him, wondering how he could fail to appreciate the provocation I had been under. Father simply stared back, and eventually I mumbled my apologies.

Then Father turned to Lily. 'What you said to Nathan just now was unfair, Lily,' he reprimanded her. 'He was very brave last night.'

'Yes, though maybe not quite so brave as Aldo,' she smiled sweetly.

'You weren't there,' I growled at her. 'You have no idea what it was like in that room.'

'Then tell us, dear cuz,' she teased.

'There's nothing to say!' Aldo said quickly.

'Except for an apology,' said Father. 'I'm waiting, Lily!'

'Sorr-eee, Nathan!' she said petulantly.

There was an uncomfortable silence around the table, broken eventually by Mrs Rathborn. 'Well, *I* thought you were very brave, Nathan,' she said. But this attempt at boosting my spirits only made me feel worse. I had been far from brave, and everyone knew it. For all my reputation as a hard fellow with my fists, I had been an utter coward when confronted with the macabre events in the library. I could feel Mrs Rathborn's and Father's concerned eyes on me, and the sense of being regarded as the poor, fragile victim of last night's fracas irked me. Mrs Rathborn demonstrated her true feelings with her next words. 'However brave you two have been,' she said to us, 'I insist that you do *not* try to confront him again tonight. He is clearly a dangerous character and not someone to be trifled with. I, for one, feel comforted by the knowledge that our uninvited guest is, at least, corporeal, and I thank you young men for proving that. Now, let him do his worst. I refuse to live in fear any longer. And when the police can be summoned, be it tomorrow or the day after, I'm sure they will catch him and remove this accursed man from our lives.'

After lunch, Father and Daniel adjourned to Daniel's study to deal with some legal matters relating to my father's company. Lily suggested a walk in the grounds, but Mrs Rathborn declined, claiming fatigue. Bonnie was then summoned from the servants' hall and the four of us put on our coats, scarves and hats and set forth on our stroll. The flakes had stopped falling by now and the snow underfoot was crisp and powdery. We had to shield our eyes from its dazzling brightness as the sun emerged into clearer skies. The snow on the lawn was pristine, until our footprints marked it.

I was quiet and introspective during much of the walk. Still angry at Lily, I could not trust myself to be civil to her, so I said little. Bonnie, as ever, was full of chatter, offering us all the latest below-stairs gossip. Alice Birch was, we learned, being courted by the assistant at the village post office. And Sara Teltree's aunt had recently suffered a fall and was currently in the hospital in Hertford. Both maids, for their different reasons, were extremely frustrated at being cut off up here at the hall on their day off.

'Oh, but it has been hard on those girls this past month,' said Bonnie. 'Not only the death of the master, and all the upheaval that has wrought, but also these dreadful noises each night. And from what they tell me, even before the master's death Gravewood was a far from peaceful place...'

'What do you mean, Bonnie?' prompted Lily.

'The arguments, my lady, between the master and his son, they often raged for hours – so said Alice.'

'Arguments?'

'Oh yes. Raised voices, threats, curses. Turned the air blue with their language, she told me.'

'Do you know what they argued about?' asked Lily, seemingly fascinated by these revelations.

'They couldn't be certain, my lady, but they reckoned it was mostly about matters concerning the legal practice. It seemed Mr Daniel was most impatient with his father about something or other, but the master was, they say, a very stubborn character.'

We were walking along the winding track between the hedgerows, mulling over this information, when Aldo suddenly fired a question at Lily and me: 'The death of John Rathborn. What do we know about it?'

I tried to recall my father's mentioning of it to us a few weeks earlier. 'Some kind of seizure, wasn't it?' I frowned.

'Tetanus, according to the coroner,' recalled Lily. 'Most likely contracted through a rusty nail.'

'Was he healthy before that?' Aldo asked.

'I believe so,' I said. 'Why?'

'He thinks Daniel Rathborn killed his father,' said Lily. 'So he could take control of the firm. Don't you, Aldo? Admit it.'

'Just exploring possibilities,' he smiled mysteriously.

'Yes, well you can put that one right out of your head,' said Lily. 'Daniel Rathborn is a fine, upstanding man of impeccable moral character. He is not a murderer, and this is not a murder investigation. We're trying to identify a nocturnal prowler, that's all. Anyway,' she added, after a pause, 'you can't kill someone with tetanus. It's a disease. Mr Rathborn was simply unlucky.'

Suddenly I noticed where we were. I stopped and turned to face the house, quickly identifying my bedroom window on the right-hand side of the first floor, beneath one of the tall, steeply sloping roofs. 'This place where we're standing is where the woman was,' I told them. 'The one I saw from my window.'

'You must have been mistaken,' said Lily, peering at the snow. 'There are no tracks here of any kind – not even deer tracks.'

I tramped across the path and looked through the hedge, searching for a lodge or small building, but saw nothing but fields. 'I'm positive I saw her,' I said. 'A lady in a black cloak.'

'Oh, please don't, Master Nathan,' said Bonnie. 'My nerves are in shreds as it is without hearing about ghostly ladies in black cloaks who leave no footprints!'

Lily glanced back towards the bedroom window. 'From this distance, it could have been anything,' she concluded. 'A dark-feathered bird – a raven, maybe.'

'Omen of death,' Aldo muttered.

'What?' squawked Lily.

'Master Aldo is right,' said Bonnie, shuddering. 'It's the old saying: "Spy a raven in the snow, die before the next cockcrow."'

'Superstitious nonsense, Bonnie,' declared Lily. 'I expect better from you.'

'You're so right, my lady,' said Bonnie. 'Think nothing on it, Master Nathan. Just silly old superstition and not worth losing a wink of sleep over... But was the snow falling, though, at the time you saw it?'

'Yes, but –'

'Oh dear,' Bonnie shivered, looking at me as though at a man on his way to the gallows. She surreptitiously crossed herself.

'But it wasn't a raven,' I protested.

'Whatever it was you saw, brother, take care,' said Aldo. 'While standing here, I have felt a vibration from the future, and it smelled of death.'

At five o'clock, we took afternoon tea in the drawing room with Mrs Rathborn. Daniel and Father remained engaged with business matters in the study. Father was in the process of acquiring a small London publisher of 'penny dreadfuls', and Daniel was helping him with the legal aspects of the purchase.

Mrs Rathborn again expressed her gratitude to Aldo and myself for exposing the mystery of the noises. She spoke as if the affair was all but dealt with, when we knew this to be far from the case. 'You boys have done your bit,' she said. 'Now we can leave it to the police to catch this trespasser.' The more she said in this vein, the more frustrated I grew. Why did she assume that *I* – a fit young man not far short of eighteen, who had proved myself as a fighter on numerous occasions, both bare-knuckle and under the Queensberry Rules – could not handle this deranged yokel with a bag over his head? If I could only rid myself of my ridiculous fear of phantoms and see the challenge essentially as a pugilistic one, then I could solve this entire case – and simultaneously restore my reputation – in one clean, knockout blow.

No sooner had this thought occurred to me than I resolved to carry it through. I would not tell anyone of my scheme, not even Aldo. This evening I would go to bed as normal, then rise just before midnight and venture downstairs to the hallway, where I would conceal myself in the shadows outside the entrance to the library. The intruder, when he appeared at his regular time of midnight or just after, would be out for the count before he knew what had hit him.

'Oh, I will be so glad to put all this behind me,' Mrs Rathborn continued. 'It has been very hard for us this past year. To be candid with you, we've had a few financial difficulties. I'm afraid my husband, God rest his soul, was a little neglectful of business towards the end of his life. Daniel is now trying to put this right, and your father has been very supportive, for which he has our unending gratitude. But, as you can see, this house requires a substantial investment simply to bring it up to an agreeable level of comfort, and it will be some while before we are in a position to make that kind of investment.'

'Your son seems a very capable man,' volunteered Lily. 'I am sure he will turn things around in the not-too-distant future.'

'I do hope you're right, my dear,' twinkled Mrs Rathborn. 'I know Daniel can appear aloof, but one must remember that it has been a difficult time for him, too, this past year, watching the practice slowly deteriorate, and then losing his father. He loved his father dearly, though he lost some faith in his professional abilities towards the end, I think it's fair to say. You are right that he is a very competent young man and is doing well now that he is in control of the firm, albeit in circumstances none of us would have wished. His dedication is a wonderful thing, but sometimes I wonder whether he is just a little too immersed in his work. He has always been very serious, even as a boy. But a man of his age ought to be giving some thought to finding a wife and starting a family, don't you think so, Lily? After all, these things don't happen by themselves, as Mrs Haverhill often says when speaking of household matters.'

'I dare say you are right,' said Lily, flushing a little. 'And, to paraphrase my uncle, I'm sure that when the right young lady makes herself apparent to him, he will be sufficiently distracted by her to put aside his legal papers, for a short while at least, and be reminded that there is more to life than work.'

'How well you put things, my dear,' laughed Mrs Rathborn. 'If you don't mind me saying so, I believe that someone with your perception and wit would make me a very fine daughter-in-law. I do so miss intelligent female company since I have been living here. How fine it would be to take tea with someone such as yourself each afternoon, as we are doing now, and converse about whatever trifling things came into our heads.'

The colour in Lily's cheeks deepened, and I couldn't help deriving some enjoyment at her discomfiture after what she had put me through at luncheon. 'How fine indeed,' she said, taking a quick sip of her tea. 'And I am most honoured that you should think so. Though I am sure there are plenty of women more worthy than I of fulfilling that role.'

Again Mrs Rathborn laughed. 'You are far too modest, Lily Morelle.'

We retired to our rooms at nine o'clock that evening. After getting into bed, I began various strategies for staying awake. First, I listened intently to the clock chimes, counting off the minutes. When I grew weary of that, I tried naming the colonies and dominions of the Empire, but got lost or bored somewhere between Sarawak, Brunei and North Borneo. In the light of a candle I checked my pocket watch. It wasn't yet eleven o'clock, and I was feeling sleepy. I had to find another means of staying awake. So I lay back and tried listing all my fights, in sequence, including the dates and names of my opponents.

I had been boxing, since the age of twelve, representing St Paul's at inter-school tournaments. I had won twenty-nine bouts out of thirty-five, and had four trophies to my name. The defeats were easy to remember. I only had to look at my face to see the marks left by each one, though the scars on my pride were far worse. I had refought those six losses many times in my head and – lo and behold – I always won!

My father was supportive of my boxing and had made special arrangements to allow me to continue with it even after I was taken out of school. He did it, I was sure, out of a desire to channel my destructive energies away from other, more dangerous and illegitimate forms of fighting. He hadn't been entirely successful. There was, I had to allow, a violence in me, dating from the time Mother died, and maybe even before then. Perhaps I was too quick to take offence and raise my fists when other, cooler heads might have walked away. Aldo often said he could tell when I was about to become violent. He told me that the thing we called *ourselves* didn't stop at the edges of our bodies but extended on outwards into the ether, and he could literally see the ether turning red around me when I grew angry about something. This image stuck in my head, and since then I always imagined the ether turning red around me when the delicious feeling of rage took hold. I would try sometimes to think *blue* or *pink* just to calm myself down, but it never worked – maybe because I did not want it to.

I had been lying there in my bed thinking these thoughts, when suddenly, out of the near-silence, a very distinct sound came to my ears, like a dull sort of thump. It came from somewhere in the house, possibly from downstairs. This was followed soon afterwards by a groan of pain. My body stiffened as my eyes stared wildly into the darkness. Was that a creak I now heard on the stairs? If only I could be sure that it was a human out there, I would be up like a shot and out on the landing, fists flying. But a fearful possibility kept me rooted to my bed: what if it's not? What if it's not? I knew I had to fight this fear. After all, I had wanted this. This was *my* time. Act now and I could hold my head up once again. I balled my fists, digging my fingernails into the flesh of my palms, trying to find some steel within me.

The house fell silent again, and at last I found it in myself to rise. But as I did so, another creak came, this time very close, just outside the bedroom door! The door handle began to move. The horrid sight of that movement – that inanimate thing twisting downwards – made me feel sick. I fell back on the bed and brought the sheet up into my mouth. I stared, beyond terror, as the door slowly opened and the dark of the corridor was revealed. Something whitish-grey stood there. The thing advanced into the room, and I felt myself falling, my head swimming, but somehow I clung to consciousness. A human figure was in my room – a woman, with blood flowing from her head. It – she – seemed to glide towards me. Then she stopped, staggered and fell to her knees.

'Nathan!' she called out as she fell, and with a shock of relief I realised it was Mrs Rathborn. But the relief was momentary. Something had wounded her, and that thing could still be about. I leapt from my bed and ran to her. Dressed only in a nightgown, she seemed delirious, on the point of fainting. I put my arms around her and helped her to an armchair.

'Oh, Nathan!' she whimpered. 'I was attacked! In my own house! Oh, monstrous!'

'Is he still here?' I asked her breathlessly.

'I–I don't know. But, Nathan, you must not go after him. It's too dangerous!'

But I was already halfway out the door.

'He may be armed!' she cried.

'Then I shall take my gun.'

From the table I grabbed the gun Williams had given to me. No longer fearful of anything but the possibility that my quarry had already fled, I ran along the corridor and half-tumbled down the staircase, made a swift turn about the huge central post at the base of the staircase, and galloped down the hallway towards the glimmer of light coming from the library. As I barged into the room I saw him, beneath the illuminated pendant lamp, in the act of tipping over the library table – a great bear of a figure, dressed in a grey cloak, with his head hidden beneath a large, shapeless bag. The table crashed to the floor in slow motion after he had let it go, and the books displaced on top seemed to hang suspended for whole minutes in mid-air. Many flew open as they fell, skidding across the wooden floor, then bouncing up again like ducks belly-flopping on a frozen pond. The noise of the table's fall echoed through the house and, after what seemed like an age, the figure finally turned to face me. His bag-head had two holes for eyes, and these black holes seemed to study me with a barely suppressed violence that was quite terrifying. I am a fairly big fellow, yet I felt puny next to this figure, who stood well over six feet, with a massive chest. I could see, beneath his voluminous cloak, his shoulders heaving breathlessly, but his head was very still.

I raised my gun and pointed it at the giant.

'Stop!' I heard my thin, scared voice say. 'Stop where you are, or I'll shoot.'

Then the demon roared. His body seemed to expand as the brawny arms beneath his cloak rose outwards like wings. He charged at me, bellowing as he came, until his voice and his physical mass seemed to block out my world. He was like death enveloping me, and that prophecy of Aldo's echoed in my ears.

I felt the impact of his big, powerful hands shoving into my chest, and I fell back helplessly against a bookcase. He grabbed me, his grip crushing my shoulders, and I smelled his hot, reeking breath on my face. The stench of sweat and desperation returned me in that instant to the fighting arena. I was like an animal cornered, and getting angrier. The ropes of muscle in my arms and legs quivered with electric energy. I erupted towards him. Suddenly, a gunshot cracked the air and everything stopped. The strength went out of his hands and he slumped silently to the floor like the water of a great wave sliding passively back into the ocean. I saw the smoke rising from the muzzle of my revolver, and the realisation of what I'd done hit me like a physical blow.

It took me some seconds to appreciate that others had gathered. Aldo, Lily and Father, and some of the servants were there at the doorway to the library, looking at me, the gun and the felled colossus with the dark red hole in his chest.

Father was the first to react. He knelt by the body and removed the bag from the head. The revealed face was large and crudely formed, with a full handlebar moustache, a red-tipped nose and thick, bloody lips that hung slackly open. The grey, bloodshot eyes were also wide open, but empty of life.

As father moved his ear to the man's chest to listen for a heartbeat, there came a shriek from Alice Birch. 'Oh my good Lord!' she cried. 'It's Richard Culpin!'

'And he's dead,' pronounced father.

CHAPTER

6

aniel arrived while we were all still standing there, and Father explained to him what had happened. Without even a glance at me, he asked to check the body for himself. Satisfied that the trespasser was dead, he then despatched Johnson, the groom, through the snowbound roads to Hertford, to summon the police and the local coroner. Meanwhile, Alice and Sara, under the supervision of an ashen-faced Mrs Haverhill, tended to Mrs Rathborn, washing and dressing the wound to her forehead. Aldo, Father, Daniel, Lily and I convened in the parlour to await the police. We were served hot chocolate by Mrs Partridge, the cook.

'Well, here's a turn-up,' commented Daniel, warming himself by the newly stoked fire.

'Indeed,' grunted father.

'Most decidedly,' nodded Aldo.

I was too stunned to add any further banalities of my own.

Happily, Mrs Rathborn was not too badly injured, as I discovered when Williams summoned me to her chamber at around one o'clock that morning. She was reclining on her bed, her back propped up with cushions, her head neatly bandaged in a style not dissimilar to Aldo's. She told me she felt an urgent need to explain her actions earlier that night. I said it was not necessary and could happily wait until morning, but she insisted on telling me the story of how she came in such a state to my room.

'Please come closer,' Mrs Rathborn urged, and I came and sat on the chair by her bed. 'I awoke in the night feeling terribly thirsty,' she said to me. 'And finding my jug empty and not wishing to trouble a servant, I decided to go down to the kitchen myself for a glass of water. But in the darkness of the hallway, someone rushed up and viciously clubbed me. I don't know how I managed to climb back up the stairs after that, but somehow I found my way to your room. The last thing I wanted was to involve you, Nathan.' Her thin, cold hand reached out and tightly clasped mine. 'I didn't want to put you in danger. But I was so scared, I didn't know what to do. I couldn't just go back to my bed, knowing that beastly man was still down there.'

'You did the right thing, Mrs Rathborn,' I told her, pretending a calm I scarcely felt. In fact I was all turmoil within. *I have killed a man,* I kept repeating to myself. *I am a murderer.* I had visions of a public trial, with witnesses queuing up to tell the world what a hot-tempered and violent reprobate I was, and how they had always known I was a bad 'un.

'You were very brave, Nathan,' she said to me for the second time in twelve hours, and once again I felt anything but. 'You mustn't feel at all bad about what you have done. I should have guessed our nightly prowler was Richard Culpin. He was a rogue and a scoundrel, and the world is a better place without him.'

'Did you know him, then?'

'Not exactly. But he used to be a tenant here. When my father died two years ago and my husband and I decided to move in, we gave Culpin notice. It must have come as something of a shock to the man. I believe he'd got it into his head that he had some sort of right to the place, having lived here for a few years. My husband did everything to persuade the man to leave. Only when he threatened to serve him with a writ of possession from the court, which would have led to his being forcibly evicted, did Culpin finally go. He left like a thief in the night, not telling us or anyone. It was a most unpleasant affair, especially when we entered the property and were able to view at first hand the squalor in which the man had lived and the damage he had inflicted on our inheritance.

'He sounds a terrible man,' I sympathised. 'You must have been nervous in those first few weeks after you moved in.'

'Yes, it's true, I was frightened for a while that he might try to continue making a nuisance of himself. But we didn't hear from him again, and I began to relax. I was wrong to do so. Evidently he's been biding his time, no doubt nursing his resentment with copious quantities of drink, before embarking on this vengeful campaign. I'm sure his plan was to scare us away from the house so that he could come and live here again. With the death of my husband he saw his opportunity, when we were at our weakest and most vulnerable. I'm sure he intended us to think his bangs and crashes were my husband's ghost returned to haunt us.'

I wanted to feel reassured by Mrs Rathborn's words, and agree with her assessment that the world was a better place without Richard Culpin. Yet I couldn't help feeling that he had been more of a victim than a scoundrel in all this. What had the man actually done? After being turfed out of his home, he'd waited two years, then gone back and trespassed a few times. He hadn't killed or seriously injured anyone. He hadn't even damaged the property. I wanted – needed – more evidence of villainy to feel better about what I'd done. I thought again about Culpin's other connection to Gravewood Hall – Polly O'Brien – and wondered what part, if any, she had played. Perhaps Mrs Rathborn knew something. I realised I had to tread carefully here, remembering the rumours of the baby's paternity.

'Mrs Rathborn,' I said warily, 'I understand that a former servant of yours lived with Culpin for a time. I don't suppose she was mixed up in this?'

'Oh, do you mean Polly?' exclaimed Mrs Rathborn. 'I'd almost forgotten about all that. Yes, well I suppose you might call that the first occasion when Culpin trespassed on our property, by dallying with one of our servants! The man was a menace in so many ways, and she was a very foolish girl. She must have learned her lesson, though. Losing her position here and then having to move in with such a pig could not have been pleasant. In fact, I understand she moved out soon after the child was born.'

Mrs Haverhill entered the room, carrying a hot milky drink on a small silver tray. 'I think it's high time you got some sleep, my lady,' she advised.

'I'm not sure I can, Mrs Haverhill.'

'I've put a few drops of chloral hydrate in your milk, which should send you off nicely,' said the housekeeper, placing the tray on the bedside table. She gave me a glare that was easy to interpret, and I bade goodnight to Mrs Rathborn.

By the time I returned to the parlour, my own hot drink was stone cold, and only Aldo and Father remained of the original party, the others having gone to bed.

'The roads are still very hazardous,' said Father. 'The police will probably not get here till morning. You two may as well take yourselves off to bed, if you wish to be of any use to anyone tomorrow.

'Before I go, Father,' I said. 'Please reassure me that I won't get into trouble over this.'

'You have nothing to worry about, Nathan. From what Daniel has told us, this Culpin fellow had a history of drunkenness and violence. The man was a serial trespasser who had only just assaulted Mrs Rathborn and, the previous night, Aldo. If anything, you should receive a medal for what you did tonight.'

'Yes, but will the police see it that way? It might be hard to prove that I acted in self-defence, given that I was armed and he was not.'

'I arrived seconds after you, brother' said Aldo, 'and I saw everything. The man charged at you with serious intent to harm.'

'But did he really, Aldo?' I demanded. 'Did he really have serious intent to harm? I know you can see colours in the ether around people's bodies that tell you about their state of mind. Well, what did you see around Culpin as he charged at me?'

Aldo merely shrugged. 'What does it matter?' he said. 'What would it prove? All that matters is how it appeared to *you*. That's all the court will be interested in, if it ever comes to court, which I doubt.'

'It matters to me,' I said, slumping back in my chair.

'The ether', said Aldo slowly, 'was pulsing red and black.'

'And what does that mean?'

'It means he meant you harm,' he said in a flat voice, without meeting my eyes. Then he bade us goodnight and left the room.

The following morning, at half past nine, I was woken by Williams and informed that my presence was urgently required in the drawing room. Blearily, I dressed and went downstairs. Waiting for me there were Daniel and my father. With them were three others, introduced to us as Inspector Jonah Simmons and Constable Henry Moss of the Hertfordshire Constabulary, and the county's Assistant Coroner, Mr Edward Ebury.

At Inspector Simmons's request, I followed the two police officers into the parlour, where I made a statement, jotted down in a notebook by Constable Moss. I described as honestly and as fully as I could the events leading up to Culpin's death, including the encounter on the previous evening. Then I walked the route with them from my bedroom to the library, explaining again what had happened. I hoped I had impressed the police officers with my testimony. I told them how fearful I was of this character, following the assaults on Aldo and Mrs Rathborn, and when he rushed at me, I had genuinely believed I was about to be killed andhad simply panicked. Later, when Aldo and Mrs Rathborn appeared, they went off separately to give their versions of the events.

For all his solemnity and the pedantic nature of his questions, I thought I could discern something in Inspector Simmons's manner to give me cause for hope. The policeman's expression, beneath his muttonchop whiskers, seemed kindly and well-disposed towards me, especially once he had heard what Aldo, Mrs Rathborn and the servants had to say. I felt he had already made up his mind what kind of man Richard Culpin was, and no doubt he would go from here to the village where he would hear more to corroborate the image he was building of the deceased, and this could only help my cause.

Mr Ebury said he would be asking a pathologist to carry out a post-mortem examination of the deceased, and there would be an inquest in a few weeks' time, which we would be required to attend. The roads were still too icy for a wagon to get through to transport the body to the Hertford morgue, so it was agreed that the corpse should be temporarily stored in a barn on the grounds of the hall. The body was wrapped in a cotton mattress cover and a thick sheet of canvas, then bound with two leather belts. It took the combined strength of PC Moss, Johnson, the groom, and James, my father's valet, to move the giant corpse to the barn. Shortly afterwards, the officials took their leave.

Later that morning, Daniel invited me into his study, a cold, gloomy place dominated by a giant tombstone of a desk. The walls were lined with shelves filled with files and large volumes of case law. He looked down his nose at me in his usual frosty fashion. 'Take a seat, Nathan,' he said, and I did so. 'As you'll remember,' he said. 'I was against the idea of arming you two, and for good reason, as it turns out. Well, never mind. We are where we are. And it could have been a great deal worse. Due process must be followed in this as in all cases. Yet, unless I'm very much mistaken, it is unlikely you will face any charges for what you did last night.'

'I'm most relieved to hear it,' I said. Actually, I felt euphoric.

'In 1824,' said Daniel, 'a chap named Scully faced a charge of manslaughter for shooting a trespasser. In that trial the judge ruled that if the accused considered that his life was in actual danger, then he was justified in shooting the deceased. The jury acquitted him. That is the legal precedent that has been followed ever since in cases like these. If you believed the man was about to kill you, then you were within your rights to act as you did.' He examined me suspiciously. 'Of course, only *you* can know the truth about that, but looking at the circumstances, and the character of the deceased, it seems that the police can only conclude that you were within your rights.'

It struck me only after I had left his study that Daniel Rathborn had not expressed a single word of gratitude or apology during the course of our conversation. He had spoken to me as a lawyer advising a client, with no acknowledgement of his own involvement in the case. He had been wrong from the outset with his theory about rats, and once it became evident that the trespasser was a man, he had not lifted a finger to help Aldo or me. In fact if he had had his way, we would have confronted the intruder unarmed. The man lacked all decency and honour, yet for some reason he was someone Lily appeared happy to encourage as a potential suitor.

There was no more snow that day, but the temperature remained icy cold, with no sign of a thaw. My father was keen to return to London, but the roads were thick with ice, and we had little choice but to accept another night's hospitality at Gravewood.

The wind really did howl that night, just as it might have done in one of my stories. It rattled at the windows like a doom-monger warning us of trouble ahead.

There was no chance of a settled night for me – no measure of contentment at a job done and a mystery solved. I knew there was more – much more – to all this than a dead bricklayer named Richard Culpin.

I dreamed I was standing in a graveyard, and the ground beneath my feet seemed to groan and shiver. Cracks appeared in one of the stones and Culpin's body broke through. His flesh had partly rotted, so that a good many of his bones were visible, yet a spirit still animated him. His eyes stared and his skeletal hand rose up beseechingly like the branch of that dead tree. 'Help me!' he cried. Then his face became dark, his eyes turned red and his index finger stretched accusingly in my direction: 'Murderer!' he screamed.

I awoke in a sweat. The wind had dropped. But the night was far from still. There was something in the air – a low groaning that had its genesis somewhere deep within the house. It was the same sound that had worked its way into my dream as the shivering ground of the graveyard. The flickering candlelight showed ten minutes past one o'clock. There were voices in the passage outside my room. I immediately got up and donned my dressing gown. In the corridor I found Lily and Aldo with their own candles, waiting for me.

'Come on,' whispered Lily, and I followed them down the stairs.

In the hallway, Lily hesitated. The groaning had stopped. 'Where did it come from?' she whispered.

'Where it always comes from,' I told her. 'The library.'

'No!' said Aldo. 'It came from deeper. The basement. Come on!'

Lily followed him and I watched the two of them disappear down the steps that led to the kitchen and the servants' hall. I nearly followed them. I would have done, except that at that moment something shadowy crossed the borders of my vision. I raised my candle and in its glow I saw a figure moving slowly along the hallway in the direction of the library. In the gloom it appeared to be a woman in a black cloak. She was carrying some bundle or other, which she held close to her chest. I was about to call out, thinking it was Mrs Haverhill or one of the maids. But there was something wrong with her, and my body, being a few seconds ahead of my thoughts in this perception, failed to respond to my commands. My lips wouldn't open, and my tongue pressed itself hard against my teeth. I couldn't say precisely what was wrong. Perhaps it was just the fact of her, at this hour, dressed as if for the outdoors, crossing the entrance hall. Where had she emerged from? Where was she walking with such silent purpose in the dead of night? And why did her feet make no sound on the tiles? These questions occurred only later. While I stood there, I instinctively felt a sense of wrongness, and that awareness immobilised me. Before I could move again, the figure had passed out of range of my candle and moved on towards the rear of the house.

My mind was still digesting this and attempting to recompose itself when I discovered, to my shock, that I was following her! I did not know how this began or what had caused me to do so. Too dazed to stop, I walked as in a dream along the hall. At the extremities of vision, where moving shadows melded into darkness, I could see her, this tall, grey woman, making her way towards the library. Some part of me had known this would be her objective – the seat of everything strange and unnatural about this house.

She paused at its entrance, and turned. I drew closer and my candle illuminated her profile. I saw the soft, round contour of her cheek, the tilt of her small nose, the sad swell of her lips. Above all I saw her extreme pallor. Her skin was chillingly white, like bleached bone or dead coral, and its whiteness made yet more vivid the startling redness of the strand of hair that had escaped the shadow of her hood and fallen across her cheek.

She did not see me, was not aware of me. Her attention was on the bundle she carried, which I now saw was a baby. After a brief pause, her head rose and she looked about her, over her shoulder towards the morning room, and then back up the hall towards me. Our eyes should have met then, but they didn't. Hers, grey-green with hints of amber, wobbled fearfully, but stared straight through me. Then she passed into the library and out of my sight.

Again, without any conscious decision to do so, I found myself following in her footsteps. At the entrance to the library I saw her from behind, moving swiftly towards the large fireplace in the south wall. When she got there, she crouched so as to step into the hearth. My astounded eyes then witnessed her continue onwards to the back of the fireplace, where she passed through the brick wall and disappeared from view.

CHAPTER

7

t was strange,' I said to Aldo the next morning. 'Unearthly strange. Even now I can't be sure I didn't dream it.'

Aldo had pulled the armchair up close to my bed where I was sitting. He was leaning forward in the chair, his brown eyes wide and staring up at me.

'You didn't dream it, brother,' he said.

'I'm amazed I wasn't scared out of my wits.'

'You were in an unusual state,' he said. 'Shocked into it, no doubt, by the sight of the apparition. Last time, you fainted. This time your mind operated a different kind of anaesthetic: it became completely passive, and let your body take over… But what you saw, Nathan, sounds like a magic lantern show. There was no sense of occupying the same space and time as this woman. Am I right?'

'No sense at all,' I said. 'She looked right through me as if I wasn't there. It was almost as though I was watching something that had already happened. Like a... visual echo. But it must have happened before there was a fireplace or a wall on that side of the library, because she went straight through it as if it wasn't there.'

'Mrs Rathborn should be able to tell us about that,' said Aldo. 'She lived here as a girl, remember?'

'She will ask us why we're asking,' I said.

'And we shall tell her,' he replied. 'It's time we told the whole truth about our experiences since we've been here at Gravewood Hall. It's our only hope of getting its residents to give up their secrets.'

The thaw had begun overnight, and Johnson reported that the roads were almost clear of ice, though perilously slippery with mud. At breakfast, father suggested that we aim to make our departure that afternoon.

'But our work isn't finished here,' I cried. 'Did you not hear the sounds last night?'

It turned out that no one, apart from Lily, Aldo and me, had heard the sounds.

'Are you sure it wasn't the wind, my dears?' suggested Mrs Rathborn. 'It was very blustery.'

'It almost certainly *was* the wind, Mrs Rathborn,' said Lily. 'We found it to be strongest in the basement. Although we failed to find the source, I'm sure the noise was made by the wind coming through a crack in one of the doors or walls.'

'It wasn't the wind,' said Aldo firmly. 'We checked every room. The only access to the outside is in the coal cellar, and both cellar doors were shut and bolted. The sound was coming from inside the basement – from one of the rooms.'

'It's rats, I keep telling you!' said Daniel.

'Could it have been rats?' Father asked Aldo and Lily.

'No!' said Aldo with some impatience. 'Rats do not groan.'

'Lily?'

She swallowed and shook her head a little sadly. 'If I'm to be honest, I would have to say it wasn't rats. The sound was like a very deep moaning. I can understand, Mrs Rathborn, how you might have mistaken it for a human sound. But I'm certain it was the wind getting in somewhere. It may not have been through the cellar doors, but some crack or crevice in the wall. I propose that we go down there after breakfast and inspect the basement very carefully, room by room. Somewhere we will find the source of that sound.'

Mrs Rathborn started to say that she thought this a splendid idea, but she was immediately interrupted by Aldo.

'I'm afraid that would be a complete waste of time!' he said starkly.

'How so?' asked Father.

'Because what we are dealing with here has nothing to do with the weather or rodents or faulty plumbing. Mrs Rathborn, you invited me here to investigate your problem, and I can say to you now that the sounds you've been hearing during the hours of darkness have no earthly origin. This house, madam, is haunted!'

Daniel began a slow handclap. 'Bravo, my young friend!' he smirked. 'You have told my mother exactly what she's been dying to hear!'

Aldo looked disdainful. 'I have no interest, sir, in what Mrs Rathborn does or does not wish to hear. I am simply stating the truth!'

'The truth!' cackled Lily. 'How wantonly you make use of that word. Do you speak of scientific truth? Truth that has been proved through the objective assessment of evidence and experiment? Or is this the truth of mediums and spiritualists, for whom something is true merely because they declare it to be so?'

'I could talk to you about the disturbances I have felt in the ether since entering this house,' said Aldo, who had now risen to his feet and was addressing the rest of us like a stage conjurer holding forth to an audience. 'But I know this will cut little ice with Lily or Mr Rathborn. So I shall speak instead of what Lily likes to call *physical evidence* – the evidence of our senses. Three nights ago, during our vigil in the library, Nathan and I distinctly heard a third person in the room. Our ears, our *physical* ears, picked up the sound of that person's breathing. There was nobody in there at the time other than the two of us. Yet we both heard it.'

He flung out a finger towards me. 'Last night,' he said in dramatically hushed tones, 'while Lily and I were in the basement, Nathan saw an apparition of a woman. She was dressed in a black cloak and carrying a baby. He saw her with his eyes, his *physical* eyes, as she walked the length of the hall and turned into the library. He saw her cross the library and enter the fireplace, and then he watched her disappear into the brickwork at the back of the hearth. Now these are things we saw and heard. That may not be enough to meet the highest standards of scientific proof, but I would be prepared to swear on the Holy Bible in any courtroom in the land that I heard what I heard, and I'm sure Nathan would be prepared to do the same.'

I felt very proud of Aldo for saying all this. I liked his calm yet resolute tone. It made me feel stronger and more capable of facing down the Daniel Rathborns and Lily Morelles of this world.

'This is dangerous nonsense,' said Daniel, looking shocked and, perhaps, a little afraid.

'And quite ridiculous,' added Lily. 'You were both in the library a long time. The dark and the cold must have begun to play on your minds, and caused you to imagine things.'

'And the woman, Lily?' said Father. 'How does your science explain that?'

'It was very dark in the hall, and our candles emitted a feeble glow,' she pointed out. 'It may be that Nathan saw one of the maids.'

'In her outdoor wear?' I objected. 'At one o'clock in the morning?'

'It's more plausible than what *you're* suggesting,' said Lily robustly. 'We should question the servants about their movements last night.'

'You may question the servants about their movements,' sighed Aldo. 'You may search for cracks in the basement wall. But you'll be wasting your time. These visitations have no earthly origin.'

'Utter balderdash,' said Daniel.

'What do you think of all this, Mrs Rathborn?' asked Father.

Mrs Rathborn looked a little pale and shaken following Aldo's speech. 'I had rather hoped,' said she, 'that our nights would once again be tranquil, following the death of Richard Culpin. It seems this is not the case. Well, all I will say is that this is an old house, and old houses tend to have ghosts. But this ghost you describe seems a quiet and peaceful sort, and I'm sure the best thing would be to leave it to its business. Mr Carter, I know you are keen to return to London today for your work, and you must go, along with Aldo, Nathan and Lily. I cannot tell you how grateful I am to you all for what you have done during your short stay here. But I am confident that with the Culpin menace disposed of, we will be fine here now. We will see you again very soon, of course, at the inquest, and we would be delighted if you would come back here afterwards for refreshments, so that we can fill you in with all the latest news of our ghost.'

The confidence of Mrs Rathborn's words was not matched by her nervous delivery of them, nor by her wan and tremulous demeanour. For all his stated desire to be gone, Father was concerned enough to respond: 'Mrs Rathborn, despite what you say, it seems to me that our work is not yet done here. I know you are only thinking of me in encouraging us to leave today, but please do not trouble yourself about any of that. My business is in capable hands, and any difficulties on that score will keep for another day or so. Your needs are far greater. Rest assured, Aldo, Nathan and Lily will get to the bottom of this mystery. And even if I have to make my departure later this week, I am happy to leave the younger ones here for as long as it takes them to finish the job.

'Mr Carter,' said Daniel. 'With all due respect, you heard my mother –'

'It's alright, Daniel,' croaked Mrs Rathborn, placing a frail hand on her son's arm. 'If Mr Carter and his family are willing to stay, then how can we object?'

'Thank you, Mrs Rathborn,' said Father. 'So, to business. Despite Aldo's objections, I agree with Lily that a practical approach is necessary in this case, if only to eliminate any possibility of natural causes. And that means a thorough search of the basement for sources of this noise, as well as another round of interviews with the servants to see if we can identify which, if any, was Nathan's ghost. Lily, why don't you enlist Bonnie and Williams to check the basement, while Aldo and Nathan interview the servants. You can use the back parlour again. Would that be alright, Mrs Rathborn?'

'Yes, I suppose so.' Mrs Rathborn seemed in an odd kind of daze. Perhaps she had not fully recovered from the blow to the head she had received from Richard Culpin. Sara Teltree was summoned and asked to escort the lady to bed.

Before she could do so, Aldo addressed a query to her mistress: 'Mrs Rathborn, before you go, one question, if I may. As far as you know, has the south wall of the library, the one containing the fireplace, always been there?'

'Oh yes,' said the lady. 'I have known this house since I was a little girl, and that room has not been altered in my lifetime.'

After she had departed, Bonnie and Williams the butler were summoned to help Lily in her search of the basement, while Aldo and I invited the housekeeper, Mrs Haverhill, to the back parlour for the first of a new round of interviews.

Aldo took up his usual position towards the rear of the room, seemingly more interested in his pocket watch than in what was being said. The questioning was therefore left entirely to me.

Mrs Haverhill was affronted by my opening enquiry. 'I most certainly was not up or about at the time you state, young sir,' she said. 'Naturally, I was fast asleep in my bed.'

'Is there anyone among the staff who might have had cause to wander the house last night?'

'The earliest to rise is always Nancy, the kitchen maid. She gets up at five o'clock to light the oven.'

I had not yet come across Nancy, and asked Mrs Haverhill if we should be speaking to her.

'You may speak to her if you wish, sir,' she replied, 'but I doubt it will profit you any. The girl has her room in the attic and otherwise lives her entire life below stairs. She is never in the main part of the house and would have no business being there. Now, if that is quite all, I have at least a hundred errands awaiting my attention. This household will not run itself, you know!'

'We know!' I assured her.

Alice Birch, our next interviewee, likewise swore she had been in bed at the time in question. When I described what I'd seen, her eyes grew round with excitement. 'Red 'air, y' say, and a baby. Well, it sounds like Polly O'Brien.'

Polly O'Brien! I exchanged glances with Aldo, intrigued by her reappearance in our investigation.

'Can you say any more about 'er?' she asked.

'She was tall,' I said to Alice, 'with very pale skin and soft round cheeks, a small, turned-up nose and grey-green eyes with flecks of amber.'

'That's Polly!' cried Alice. 'Oh, sir, you've described 'er to a tee. But I don't understand. Beg pardon, sir, but what would Polly O'Brien be doin' wanderin' the hallway in the middle of the night when she's been gone from Gravewood this twelvemonth past, and not been seen in the village since last summer. It makes no sense, sir. No sense at all!'

'No,' I agreed. 'It makes no sense. But, Alice, I don't believe it *was* Polly I saw.'

'It sounds just like 'er, sir!'

'What I mean is, I think I saw her ghost.'

'Her ghost?' Alice gave a sudden, violent tremble. 'Then that would mean Polly's dead, sir.'

'Indeed!'

'But 'ow? I mean, scuse my askin' sir, but 'ow do you know it was a ghost?'

'I stood not three yards from her, Alice, and she looked straight through me, as if I wasn't there. And she paid equally scant regard to the wall behind the library fireplace: she simply walked straight through it, and disappeared from view. I felt I might have been watching something that had already taken place.'

'Well that's impossible, sir. For one thing, Polly never 'ad the baby while she was livin' 'ere. Li'l Jimmy was born six months after she left. So what you saw could never 'ave 'appened.'

After Alice had left us, still muttering to herself and shaking her dazed head, we summoned Sara Teltree. She limped in and sat down, looking tiny on the big armchair. Sara quickly confirmed that she had been in bed at the stated hour. She then listened as I described to her what I had seen.

When I mentioned that Alice had identified the apparition as looking like Polly O'Brien, her reaction was even more dramatic than her fellow housemaid's. Her little body became very tense and her hands fidgeted with her apron. This surprised me as she had already said she had never known Polly, and was a relative newcomer to the house.

The girl wouldn't speak, so I tried gently coaxing her. 'You seem rather nervous, Sara. Do you have anything to say?'

'No, sir,' she said. 'I'm just a little scared at the idea of a ghost in this house. I don't care for the idea of it, sir.'

'Have you ever seen a ghost here before?'

'No, sir. And I hope never to, sir.'

'You may not have seen a ghost, Sara Teltree, but you know something,' piped Aldo from the back of the room. He shut his watch with a snap and rose from his chair. 'I ask myself: why should you be frightened that Polly has come back? – this woman you claim never to have met. You know something, my girl, and you're not telling!'

He was leaning in close to Sara now, staring beadily at her, his nose inches from her face.

She cowered from him. 'Oh no, sir. Please. Have mercy. I have no knowledge of this woman. I've not been here long.'

'No, you came from the reform school, right?' he sneered. 'I'll wager you were a beggar or a thief before that, eh? Living a life of lies and deceit. Well, old habits die hard, missy. I saw through that veil of innocence the first time I laid eyes on you. Now, tell us what you know before we order a full search of your room and possessions!'

I stared, astonished and a little concerned, at this performance by Aldo. But I didn't intervene. His methods may have been rough, but they were usually effective.

Sara Teltree was crying bitterly by this stage. 'Oh, no sir,' she sobbed. 'You blacken my name most cruelly. Mine is not a happy tale, it's true. I own I made mistakes in the past, but I am not a deceitful person. My mistress showed Christian mercy in offering me a second chance and I like to think I have proved myself worthy of her kindness.'

Aldo was by now behind the girl, resting on the back of her chair and obliging her to twist in her seat to view him. 'In which case,' he said, 'why persist in lying to us now, Sara? You have something to say about Polly O'Brien, so say it.'

'Sir, I have nothing to say.'

'Then we have no choice but to order a search.'

'No sir! You cannot do that! It is not fair,' she wept.

'So tell us!' he bellowed.

She wiped her eyes and tried to compose herself. 'It's not my fault,' she said at length. 'If a piece of knowledge comes into my hands, I cannot be blamed for it.'

'Of course not,' I assured her.

'I was given Polly's old room,' she sniffed, now focusing her attention on me. 'It's a small, bare room, with a bed, a chest of drawers and a wardrobe. Nothing more.'

'Go on,' I prompted.

'The third drawer in the chest would never close properly. I don't know why, but this bothered me. So one day I took it right out, and found behind it, at the very back, a small black book.'

'What was in the book, Sara?' I asked her.

'It was a diary, sir. Polly's diary. I don't know why she left it there. Perhaps she forgot it.'

'And? Did you read the diary?'

She nodded. 'Yes, sir. My reading isn't what it ought to be, and her handwriting was hard to understand, but I made out most of it. I wish I hadn't, though. I really wish I'd never found it, for the things it contained.'

'Why? What did it contain?' I asked, scarcely able to contain my curiosity.

'Secrets, sir, about the... the old master, Mr John.'

'We've heard the rumours about Mr John and Polly,' said Aldo. 'Were they true?'

Again she nodded. 'They were true, sir. And there's more.'

'More?' I probed. 'Pray tell.'

'I cannot,' she said. 'I am ashamed to know such things, and don't feel capable of repeating them. If you are so concerned to become acquainted with these matters, it would be better if you read about them for yourselves.'

'Can you fetch the diary now, Sara?' Aldo asked.

'I will, sir. But, please, may I beg you to say nothing of my knowledge of its contents to either the master or the mistress. I would not want it known that I am aware of any of the details my predecessor saw fit to set down on paper.'

'Rest assured, we won't say a word,' I told her. 'It is the diary we are interested in, Sara. Your role in discovering it is not important, and you cannot be blamed for it.'

'Thank you, sir,' she curtsied, and was gone.

'Well, well, a diary,' I said to Aldo when the door had shut. 'And good for you for squirrelling it out of her. This could be a turning point, brother!'

'I have no doubt,' said Aldo, 'this diary will prove interesting. And there are more secrets besides, still interred in this house. The whole place stinks, and I'm not only speaking of the mildew.'

Before Sara returned with the diary, Lily entered. I guessed from her demeanour that she had not met with success.

'Nothing!' she said, sinking disconsolately into the armchair lately vacated by Sara. 'Not a chink or cranny to be found anywhere. For such a neglected house, the basement is exasperatingly robust. It seems you were right, cousin: the noise must have been generated *inside* one of the rooms. Don't ask me how. Did you have any luck finding your ghost?'

'No,' I smiled. 'But, after hearing me describe it, Alice Birch swears it's the spit of Polly O'Brien. And we've also found Polly's diary.'

'Her diary! Now that sounds interesting,' she said, already looking more cheerful.

'The second housemaid, Sara Teltree, admitted to finding it,' I said. 'Poor thing's terrified of anyone knowing she's acquainted with its secrets. So she's never read it, understood?'

'Understood,' chuckled Lily.

CHAPTER

ara returned soon afterwards. With the small black book held nervously before her in pink hands, she looked like a repentant thief returning a stolen item. When she saw Lily, she became rooted to the spot, and seemed ready to flee the room.

'Have no fear, Sara,' I told her. 'I have already assured my cousin that you know nothing of the contents of the book you are holding.' She breathed a sigh of relief, then silently handed me the diary, curtsied, and departed.

I opened it and began flicking through the pages, about half of which had writing on them. The writing was a dense, forward-slanting scrawl, divided into paragraphs, some brief but others quite expansive, with each entry headed by a date. The diary spanned the entire ten months of Polly's employment at Gravewood Hall. The first entry was dated Monday 17 January 1881, and the final entry Wednesday 16 November of the same year.

'Don't keep us waiting, cousin,' prompted Lily. 'Tell us what it says.'

'There's a lot of it,' I warned her. 'This may take some time.' I read out a sample entry from early in the diary:

Friday 28 January

Late on duty again this morning. I can't help it. I find it so hard to wake up. Mrs H was furious. She says I can't have time off this Sunday. Cruel, heartless woman! But I bit my tongue and got on with my duties. I swept out the ashes and lit the fires in the downstairs rooms, brought up heated water for the master and mistress, emptied and cleaned the chamber pots, made the beds, swept, dusted and cleaned the bedrooms, scrubbed the downstairs hallway floor and beat the rug, and all before 1 o'clock. I feel so tired. Tomorrow, I know, will be worse because of the dinner party. Mrs H shows me no mercy. She hates me. I don't know why. Perhaps because I sing to myself while I work. But if I didn't, I know I would go mad.

'Sounds like a bad day,' said Lily. 'Is it all like that?'
I read out the following entry:

Saturday 29 January

Mrs P saw me ironing the master's newspaper and
sprinkled some scent on it. 'Put the master in a
good mood,' she said. 'Make the news smell sweeter.'
How I laughed at that. Then I had to lace the
mistress in. 'Tighter, tighter,' she told me. It took
all my strength to close that corset to her
satisfaction. She seemed upset. 'So many decisions,'
she moaned, 'and never any support. Never any
support!' It wasn't my place to ask, but she does
seem a lonely lady. Come to think of it, I hardly
ever see the master and mistress in the same room
together. By the way, she said to me, we're having
company this evening. As if I didn't know. It's all
Mrs H has been talking about this week. 'Woe
betide any shirkers, malingerers and bunglers,' she
warned us. Well, we got through it. Mrs P
panicked, of course, but nothing was ruined and
nothing was spilled and no one complained. And
afterwards we all sat in the servants' hall and
listened to the master, Mr John, playing the piano
upstairs. What a lovely sound it was.

Looking a little further on, I came upon the
following entry:

Thursday 24 February

Mrs H is looking highly pleased with herself. I even caught her smiling (perish the thought!) and inspecting her appearance in the mirror on the upstairs landing when she thought no one was looking. This past week she's no longer been the unexpected creak on the stairs or the looming shadow in the hallway, catching me unawares. In fact she has scarcely been about. I wonder where she gets to these days.

'Well, well,' chuckled Aldo. 'It sounds as though Mrs Haverhill may have found herself a man.'

'Perish the thought!' said Lily.

Passing over a few mundane-looking entries, my eye fell upon this:

Tuesday 15 March

The master's secretary, Wilkins, is ill, and I said to the mistress that I would gladly fill in for him, having learned the art of Pitman shorthand from my brother. The mistress was content for me to do so, as was the master, but Mrs H was vexed with me for not obtaining her consent beforehand. She made a great show of the inconvenience my absence would cause, but this is hardly a busy time in the house. Spring cleaning isn't yet begun, and Alice and Nancy can do my duties for a day or so.

I confess that I may have had a personal motive in volunteering. The master, Mr John, is a kind man with lovely manners. And it hasn't escaped my notice that he is very handsome, despite being at least twenty years my senior.

Wednesday 16 March
Wilkins' illness persists, I'm pleased to say, and I was required to spend a further day almost exclusively in Mr J's company. It felt very pleasant sitting there among all the papers and books with Mr John. He keeps the curtains closed because of his dislike of the sun, which he says hurts his eyes. It makes the room quite cosy. I loved listening to his warm, deep voice speaking about important things. I hope I'm proving an efficient replacement. He's made no complaint so far when he reads back the letters he has dictated to me. I confess I giggle too often and for too long at some of the funny little remarks he makes on the letters he receives.

Thursday 17 March
Alas, Wilkins is recovered, and I must end my happy sojourn in Mr J's study and return to my duties in the house. Mrs H was more than usually stern with me, though I did all my duties to a high standard and in good time. I know she deplores my singing, which I own was louder than usual today.

Skipping on a few more pages, I found the following:

Monday 28 March

I find I am thinking of Mr J a great deal. When I polish the silverware, I cannot help but picture his fine, strong hands holding the spoon or fork, and when I light a fire, I often imagine him standing before it, warming himself. More than once I have found myself lingering near the door of his study, making a pretence of dusting the hallway furnishings, in the hope that I might catch a sight of him as he comes out. At times I've yielded to fantasies of myself as a lady in his own rank of life. But then in the hallway mirror I spy the red-haired girl in the drab maid's uniform, and I am dealt a reminder of the truth of my situation...

Thursday 31 March

I can't pretend otherwise any longer: I love Mr John Rathborn! There – I've said it. I know what you're thinking, dear diary. A more foolish creature was not yet born, and I quite agree! Yet how can I deny this feeling? Dearest diary, these words now inked on your pages make real this feeling which, until now, was nothing more than a beautiful ache in my heart.

Monday 4 April

I've tried – Lord knows how I've tried – to get him to look at me, but these past few days he's favoured me with only the most fleeting of glances. Most of each week he spends in his office in London, and when he's at Gravewood, he's closeted in his study with Wilkins, dictating letters, or with Mrs H, going over the weekly accounts. He's often in a poor temper, especially when his son Daniel visits, and I've often been a sad and helpless witness to their violent rows. I wish I could do something to comfort him, if I could only get him to notice me again, but it's brutally clear he doesn't need or care for me. I've cried myself to sleep these past few nights, remembering those two cherished days last month that I spent alone with him in his study. If he only knew what I'd give for a single kind word or smile, but why should he? This love I feel is a fault, a defect in me. However good and right it feels inside, I know it must be wrong. Mrs H has no need to complain of my singing these days, for there are no more melodies in me. I'm dead inside.

There was more in this vein – much more. I thumbed through the pages, searching for the next development in her narrative. Finally, I found this:

Thursday 21 April

Oh, sweet heaven! I'm floating on clouds. Dear diary, I can scarcely breathe for joy. Today, he smiled at me for the first time in weeks, and not only that: he spoke! The smile alone I could have happily fed off for a fortnight, but the words he said, as I served him his tea in the parlour, were the stuff of dreams. 'Polly,' he said to me, 'You have been in my thoughts lately.' I nearly spilled the cup over him when I heard this, but I managed to control myself and answer as innocently as I could: 'Have I, sir?' 'Yes,' he said. 'Wilkins resigned today. He has found a new position in London, and until I find a replacement, I would like you to act as my secretary. Will you report for duty at nine o'clock tomorrow morning?' 'Why, yes sir, but–' 'Don't worry,' he interrupted, 'I'll clear it all with Mrs Haverhill.' And that was that. I was shaking like a leaf as I left the room, and have been shaking ever since. Mrs H is white-lipped with fury. Her hatred of me has risen to new heights in the past few hours. I don't know why. She can hardly blame me for this turn of events. But Mrs H is the least of my worries. I shan't sleep tonight for thinking about tomorrow: Mr J and me, alone for six hours or more. Sweet heaven be praised! I shan't sleep!

'Stop!' said Lily. 'I beg you, no more of this pathetic woman's romantic ravings. We can guess where this sordid affair will lead. We know they have a dalliance and that she falls pregnant. Go to the end, Nathan. Let us hear how it all turns out.'

Obediently, I turned to the final entries of her diary. The handwriting had become quite ragged by this stage, with several crossings out, as if done in a hurry. I read out the following:

Thursday 10 November

I found J in the library this afternoon. This is where he spends most of his time since his son moved in last month. He likes it because it's always dark in there – the sunlight can't get through the trees just outside. I took him a pot of tea, though he hadn't ordered one. I just had to see him, and this was the only way I could think of doing so without making Mrs H suspicious. J was happy, as always, to see me. After I poured the tea, I let my hand linger by his and he took it and kissed it for a long time. The warmth of his lips on my skin was like electricity running through me. He told me he'd been thinking of me and was very glad I'd come. It made me happy but also sad to hear this for it proved that he isn't master in his own house and is as trapped as I am by the constant need for discretion. The mistress isn't the issue – hasn't been for months. In almost every way, they lead separate lives and are husband and wife in name only. The issue is their son, Mr Daniel. I've overheard enough of the quarrels between Messrs J and D to work out that Mr D urgently wishes to take over the family law firm. It seems to me that Mr D is trying to help his case by seeking evidence of his father's lapsed morals. To this end, he has enlisted Mrs H as his chief spy, which would explain why she's so often on my tail. They both suspect us, but have no proof as yet. The proof they seek is, of course, growing larger inside me every day. Soon I will no longer be able to hide it behind a loosely belted apron. My only hope is that J will be able to think of some way through our predicament before that day arrives. But first I have to find the courage to tell him of the predicament. I daren't think how he will react, nor what it will mean for myself and the little baby for whom I already feel such love.

'So now Mrs Haverhill is Mr Daniel's spy,' sighed Lily. 'This woman seems to think she is a character in a melodrama. She has completely lost touch with reality!'

I read on:

Friday 11 November

Diary, I've told him! It took all my nerve. Again, the setting was the library, and once again I had brought him tea – unasked for. I was desperately scared as I spoke the words. I know that J is a kind man and has told me many times that he loves me, but here I was testing that love as never before – presenting him with a predicament that will bring him nought but scandal and disgrace, and this at a time when his business is struggling and he's fending off the ferocious ambition of his son. His only choice, I understood, was to hush it up. And yet a part of me dared hope that he might react differently – that he might even see this as a sign that our love was meant to be. Well, sweet diary, I'm delighted to report, my wildest hopes were fulfilled. When he heard my news, his face lit up with such a smile as I had not seen from him in weeks. He vowed there and then to love and protect me and the child to the best of his ability. He said 'It must be our secret for now, but in the fullness of time –' I stopped him there and said: 'Speaking of fullness and time, sir, I have quite a lot of the one and not much of the other, if you take my meaning.' He didn't, so I indicated my belly, and he nodded.

'You are right,' he said. 'We must act soon. But it must be handled carefully. And for the present we must be especially discreet, so perhaps you should not bring me any more pots of tea, Polly.'

Saturday 12 November

In my meeting with J yesterday, he said little, but his words were heavy with meaning, which I've been pondering over all this day. He swore he would love and protect me and the child, which encouraged me to believe that he is imagining some sort of future with myself and the little one. Am I reading too much into his words? I hope not. I've never known J to be anything but honourable with me. And yet he never did explain what he meant by 'love and protect'. It didn't exactly sound like an offer of marriage. And 'We must act soon' was vague in the extreme. I'm sure that if J is thinking of marrying me, his wife wouldn't stand in the way. No, my biggest fear in that regard is Mr Daniel, who seems bent on destroying his father's reputation so that he can win control of the family business. And this is why I must do as J says and practise discretion. No tea was delivered to the library this afternoon, and nor did I dally over my duties in the hallway in hopes of a chance encounter. How I ache to see and talk with him again, but for now I must be patient.

Sunday 13 November

I walked into the village this afternoon with Alice. She's been my closest friend during my time at Gravewood, and more than once I've been on the point of telling her my secret, but I've always held back, knowing how dangerously loose her tongue can be. So we talked of small things and complained, as usual, about Mrs H. While in the village, we met the bricklayer Richard Culpin. I didn't much care for the smell of alcohol coming off him, nor for the way he smiled and gaped at me. Though well covered in my coat, I almost felt he'd managed to divine my condition through a kind of animal sensibility. (Among the animal kingdom, Mr Culpin doesn't strike me as very far advanced beyond the level of pig.) He bowed and doffed his cap to us and bade us good morning in an exaggerated and mocking sort of way. Alice laughed and would probably have tarried a while in his company if I hadn't swiftly bustled her away.

Monday 14 November

It's happened! We've been discovered! I'm scared, yet also excited – I will know very soon what fate has in store for me. How did it happen, when we'd made such efforts to be careful? Well, for all J's talk of discretion, I must have lit a fire in his heart with my news, for he sent for me this morning.

No sooner had I entered the library than he seized hold of me and took me onto his lap. Then he placed his hand on my belly, in contact with my skin, to feel for himself the evidence of his child. I loved that he was so thrilled by it. His touch had its effect on me. I couldn't help myself. I kissed him, and he responded. While in that attitude, we were surprised by Mr D. Had he followed me there, and then listened outside the door? It's very likely, for he doesn't normally venture this far along the hallway. There he stood, at the entrance to the room, looking down his long, thin nose at us, a terrible smile playing on his lips. Then, as abruptly as he'd appeared, he was gone. By this time I was standing again, shaking uncontrollably. J took my hand, told me not to worry. His calmness was some comfort, for I knew he stood to lose far more from this than me. 'Are you not worried that he will use this to his advantage in his fight with you?' I asked. 'Let him do his worst,' laughed J. 'So I kissed a maid. What man hasn't?' 'But what about when my condition becomes known?' I pointed out. 'That will make things more difficult for you.' He smiled and stroked my cheek. 'I will deal with that when the time comes,' he said. This was less reassuring to hear, but I had no chance to question him further, for I could hear Mrs H calling and I had to return to my duties. So where does this leave me?

In the hands of two men. Will Mr D now urge his
mother to sack me? And if she does, how will I
respond? Could this be the spur he needs to finally
act on his desires, divorce his wife and marry me?
I hardly dare express the hope. It seems so unlikely.
And yet how unlikely was any of this even a few
months ago? He and I have come such a distance
since then. Why not now make that final leap?
These are my fears and hopes as I write this
evening. I'm helpless, as usual, to affect the course
of events, and must trust to God's mercy.
Tomorrow I should know the truth. Dearest diary,
I pray that the next words I write in your pages
will be happy ones.

Tuesday 15 November

Diary, you find me in a state of fearful anguish.
Mr D has chosen to use his information in a way
more cruel than I could ever have imagined. This
morning, as I was going about my duties, carrying
a basket of laundry along the first-floor landing, he
came out suddenly from his bedroom, where he
must have been lying in wait for me. He pulled me
in there and closed the door. To my horror,
he then started to kiss me forcefully on the lips.
I dropped my basket and tried to push him away,
but he grabbed my wrists and again pulled me
towards him. 'If you'll kiss my father, then why

not me?' he whispered. 'Leave me be, sir,' I pleaded,
but I was unable to prevent his embraces. In the
course of this foul and hateful episode, which I can
barely bring myself to recall, he became aware of
my swollen belly, and a dreadful smile appeared on
his lips. He leaned very close and said a truly
horrid thing: 'Lie with me,' he said, 'or I will tell all
to my mother.' He bade me come to his room at
midnight tonight, if I wanted a future here. Then
he handed me my basket and shoved me back into
the corridor. The rest of the day was spent in a
daze. My body continued to function. I walked,
kneeled, scrubbed, washed, dusted and polished, but
my mind was in turmoil. Desperately I waited for
a summons from J. His silence was agony to me.
Time and again I contemplated going to him, but
Mrs H was like a hawk, watching my every move.
Why did he not send for me? If J would only state
publicly the truth of our love, then all my troubles
would be over. But there has been no word from
him, and the time now stands very close to
midnight, the time of my appointment with his
loathsome son. Of course I won't go to him – I'd
sooner die! And tomorrow, I know I'll be dismissed.
I'll be forced to leave Gravewood and seek another
situation. But who will take me in my condition?
Surely J will act tomorrow, rather than see me
disappear from his life and sink into destitution.

I mustn't lose my faith in him. He'll find a way through all this. He'll not stand for the loss of his child, nor let the woman he loves end her days in the workhouse.

I glanced up at Lily after reading this. She was shaking her head and muttering: 'Deranged – the girl is quite deranged. This is the work of a fantasist.'

'Do you want me to continue?' I asked. 'We've reached the final entry, and it's quite a long one.'

She waved her hand carelessly. 'Ah well, I suppose we may as well see it through.'

Wednesday 16 November

I was called into Mrs H's office this morning, and she informed me that it had come to her notice that I was with child. This was, she said, an intolerable state of affairs, and the mistress had decided to terminate my employment here immediately. She spoke without emotion, but I reckoned I heard a note of quiet triumph in her voice. Numbness crept through me as I climbed the stairs to my attic room. I considered throwing myself from the window, but a gentle stirring in my belly stopped that thought. As I was packing my suitcase, there came a knock at my door. I expected it was Alice come to wish me farewell, and was startled to see J standing there. Seeing him look at me with such sadness was too much, and I burst into tears. I continued to cry, even as he held me, and I'm afraid I stained his shirt with my tears. He spoke slowly and gently to me, saying: 'I will make arrangements for you to live here within these walls. I will contact you in due course when everything is ready for your return. In the meantime you must go the house of the bricklayer, Richard Culpin. I have paid him to provide you with board and lodging for the next few months, until I send for you.' Of all the people to send me to, why Culpin? 'Does it have to be his house, sir?' I asked plaintively. 'I had to act in secrecy and haste,' he replied, 'and Culpin was the only person I could think of. He has promised to behave respectfully towards you and to provide for all your needs. I must go now, dearest. Please trust me. This will all end well, I promise you.' I began to sob again as he removed his arms from me. I'm ashamed to say I lost some self-control. 'Oh, sir!' I cried. 'Why must it be this way? We love each other. You've told me you feel no love for your wife. Why can't you divorce her and marry me?' It was the first time I'd spoken so brazenly to him of my secret hopes and desires, but I was desperate, not knowing when or whether we'd meet again. He wasn't angry, but only smiled and put his finger to my lips to hush me. Then he explained, using words I struggled at times to follow, the laws of the land and how they related to our situation. If I understood him correctly, there is no law in England that allows two people to divorce, except on grounds of adultery. As J is the wrongdoer, it would be up to his wife to seek a divorce. He told me he has begged her to do so, but she refuses, not because she loves him, which she doesn't, but because she would lose Gravewood Hall. He explained that in a divorce, all property of the marriage, including Gravewood Hall, would go to him, and, on his death, to his son Mr Daniel. Nothing would go to his wife. He has offered to gift her Gravewood Hall in the event of a divorce, but his son has threatened to sue him if he does that, as Mr Daniel doesn't wish to see his inheritance pass to his mother. He has plans to sell the property, something his mother would never consent to. When I heard this, I sank onto my bed in despair. 'So, because of a dispute over this house, you can never leave your wife,' I said. 'I did not say never,' he smiled, and went on to explain: 'A bill will shortly go before Parliament, which should become law by the end of next year. The law will give women rights over any property they brought into their marriage. This house was given to Mary by her father as part of her wedding dowry. According to this new law, it will become hers again in any divorce, and there is nothing Daniel or I or anyone else can do about it. Mary has promised she will agree to a divorce once this law comes into force. This time next year, dearest, we should be free to pursue our dream of a life together. But until that time, we must be patient and continue as best we can.' After that, he departed and I was left with a head full of questions. Chief among these was what he meant by those puzzling words: I will make arrangements for you to live here within these walls. What he is planning I cannot begin to work out. But what choice do I have but to trust him and pray that what he promises will eventually come to pass. And now I will leave off this diary to finish my packing, and thence to Richard Culpin. God have mercy on my soul!

9

'That's it!' I said to them, shutting the book with a snap.

'And we're supposed to accept these childish babblings as evidence of something, are we?' said Lily.

'If Polly is to be believed,' I frowned, 'Mrs Rathborn knew about the affair, because John discussed it with her – no doubt after Daniel told her about it. Yet when I spoke to Mrs Rathborn the night before last, she was under the impression that Richard Culpin was the father of Polly's child.'

'Who knows what was discussed and what was known?' said Lily dismissively. 'We're basing it on secondhand information from an unreliable source.

Mr John was clearly trying to placate an unstable woman, telling her what she wanted to hear. It's the usual story with men and their mistresses the world over. I'd sooner believe Mrs Rathborn than anything Polly O'Brien has to say.'

'Whatever you may think, Lily, Daniel Rathborn does not come out of this well,' I observed. 'No wonder Sara Teltree was so nervous about showing it to us.'

'The only person who doesn't come out of this well,' said Lily, 'is the diarist. I simply refuse to believe that Daniel Rathborn would ever stoop to the actions of which she accuses him. He may be ambitious, but since when was that a fault? He may have been frustrated by his father's neglect of the family business. Again, where is the blame in that? When all is said and done, he is a gentleman, and her account of the incident in his bedroom strikes me as malicious fantasy.'

'Do I detect a slight lapse in objectivity on the part of our resident scientist?' smiled Aldo. 'I can't help noticing since we have been here that you are not entirely indifferent to the charms of the young master of this house, and I make no comment on that. But are you sure your feelings for him aren't prejudicing you against Polly O'Brien's account?'

'I have no feelings for Daniel Rathborn beyond those of ordinary friendship,' said Lily, colouring a little. 'I simply dislike seeing an innocent person's character being blackened.'

'Leaving that aside,' said Aldo. 'By far the most interesting part of this diary are the twelve words that so puzzled Polly: "I will make arrangements for you to live here within these walls." What do you suppose he meant by that?'

'He must have had some plan to invite her back,' I suggested, 'perhaps as a guest rather than as a servant, once he had gained the consent of his wife and son.'

Aldo rubbed his watch thoughtfully. 'Maybe so, but it seems unlikely, doesn't it? In a small village like Winterby, people would soon talk. I can't imagine Mrs Rathborn exposing herself to such a potentially humiliating situation.'

'What then?' I said. 'Are you suggesting he had plans to re-engage her as a housemaid? With a baby? Inconceivable.'

'What do *you* think, Lily?' Aldo asked.

'Mr John was simply playing the part of all unfaithful husbands through the ages,' she said, 'whispering sweet lies to his little girlfriend. Of course he had no plans to bring her back, and the girl was an utter fool to believe that he did.'

'So what now?' I asked, after a short pause.

'We check the basement,' said Aldo.

'Again?' complained Lily. 'But I've already checked it thoroughly.'

'Yes,' he nodded, 'but you were looking for cracks in the wall. This time we'll be looking for something completely different.'

The three of us descended the stone steps to the basement, accompanied by Williams, who hobbled as fast as he could to keep up with us. This was my first visit below stairs at Gravewood. It was even gloomier than the rest of the house, and the air was thick with greasy cooking smells and coal dust. Aldo led the way, marching into the first room he came to and demanding to know where he was.

'This is the pantry, sir,' said Williams, somewhat redundantly, as the room could not be mistaken for anything else. It was lined with shelves filled with bottles, jars, and baskets of fruit and vegetables.

'And what room is directly above us?' was Aldo's next question.

'That would be the drawing room,' answered Williams.

Lily and I exchanged quizzical glances, wondering what was on Aldo's mind. We followed him through a doorway to our left, finding ourselves in the kitchen, where Mrs Partridge, the cook, was hard at work at a long wooden table, preparing the lunch. Assisting her was a thin, pale girl of no more than fifteen, who I assumed to be Nancy, the kitchen maid. At the far end of the enormous room was a large black cooking range.

'You'll excuse us, Mrs Partridge,' said Williams. 'The young masters and mistress are making another of their investigations.'

'That's quite alright, Mr Williams,' responded the cook, 'you go right ahead. Just mind yourselves on the range, which is very hot.'

'What room is above here, Williams?' asked Aldo.

The butler frowned for a moment. 'The dining room, sir.'

'Aha!' exclaimed Aldo. 'So we are now on the eastern side of the house, am I right?'

'That would be correct, sir.'

Aldo gestured towards the cooking range. 'And I am now pointing approximately north, yes?'

'Yes, sir.'

'Good! Very good!' Aldo walked to the southern end of the room, where he positioned himself beneath a shelf laden with copper pots and pans of varying sizes. He then began to pace along the floor in a straight line towards the northern end, counting loudly as he did so. 'One...two...three.' Mrs Partridge and Nancy were obliged to make way for him as he passed them. 'Eleven...twelve...thirteen,' he counted. 'Twenty paces,' he declared at the end of his journey. 'Take a note of that, Nathan.' Then he marched through a doorway to his right into the next room. 'What is this room, Williams?' he demanded.

We all hurried after him, finding ourselves in a dark, drab little room, filled with large sinks, tubs and piles of laundry.

'This is the scullery, sir.'

'And what are we beneath?'

'The master's study, sir.'

Aldo paced the room, again heading in a south-to-north direction. 'Seven paces,' he said. 'Remember, Nathan. The kitchen is twenty, and the scullery is seven.' He pointed to the scullery's southern wall. 'What room is directly behind this wall, Williams?'

'Er… that would be my office, sir.'

'Please direct us there.'

We followed Williams's bent figure back into the kitchen, and then out into the corridor by the stairs. It was slow going, following this crouching, shuffling old man as he led us north along the corridor to the servants' hall. To our right was another doorway, which led into his office. It was a spare, chilly place, with white walls, a simple chair, a desk and a tall wooden cabinet for storing papers. The only item hanging on the wall was a small photograph of a pretty young woman, who might have been Williams's daughter or long-ago lover – I didn't like to ask.

Aldo pointed at the wall on which the photograph hung. 'That is the southern wall, am I right?'

'Yes, sir.'

'On the other side of that wall is the scullery?'

'Yes, sir.'

'And above us?'

'The library, sir.'

'The library,' breathed Aldo, raising his eyebrows as if he had just discovered something quite profound.

His attention was then drawn towards the photograph on the wall. 'Your wife?' he enquired.

'No sir, I never had the good fortune to marry.' Williams bowed his head.

'So who is she, then?' asked Aldo, a touch impertinently I thought.

'I do not know, sir,' answered Williams. 'I bought the picture in a gallery shop some twenty years ago. I always thought her rather lovely.'

Aldo nodded. 'I agree with you.' Then he went and stood beneath the photograph and measured out the room. 'Five paces, Nathan,' he announced. 'Now please add it all up for me. You remember the length of the kitchen, don't you? And the scullery?

I want the total length of those two rooms added to the five paces of Mr Williams's office.'

Lily beat me to it: 'Thirty-two paces,' she said exasperatedly. 'And now you've finished measuring the house, Aldo, can you please tell us what this is all about?'

'Patience, dear girl, patience,' he replied. 'We are only halfway there.'

He departed the office, traversed the servants' hall and strode swiftly down the corridor, with the rest of us trailing in his wake. Back up the stairs we went, before crossing the hallway into the dining room.

'We are now directly above the kitchen, Williams. Am I right?'

'Yes, sir,' answered the butler a little breathlessly.

Aldo paced out the dining room. 'Fourteen paces, Nathan,' he shouted, before diving back into the hallway and thence to the study. He knocked on the door, and entered without waiting for a reply. There was no one there but Alice with her duster.

'If you're looking for the master or Mr Carter, you'll find them with Mr Johnson in the stables,' she said. 'And the mistress is in the parlour.'

'It's alright, Alice,' I said to her. 'It's the room we're interested in, not its occupants.'

'Right you are, sir,' she said, and went on with her dusting.

'Below this floor lies the scullery,' Aldo said to Williams, and the butler nodded. Aldo paced it out. 'Eight paces, brother. Please keep these figures in your head.'

We all marched out again, and followed Aldo to the library.

The others went into the room, but I remained at the threshold, a shiver running through me as I recalled the strange and tragic events I had witnessed there. Aldo paced carefully from the fireplace to the book-lined rear wall. He counted ten paces, finishing up with his nose against one of the bookshelves. 'I am now at the northern extremity of the house. Is that right, Williams?'

'Yes, sir.'

'Beneath this wall is the northern wall of your office?'

'Indeed, sir.'

'And what is the total length of the three rooms I have just paced out – the dining room, the study and the library?'

Again, Lily was quicker to the answer: 'Thirty-two paces, Aldo,' she said. 'Just as it was downstairs.' She gave him a sarcastic round of applause. 'Bravo! You have proved that the basement is the same length as the ground floor. What a remarkable conclusion! Who would ever have guessed it?'

Aldo's shoulders slumped. He turned to face us, frowning and gazing into space. He scratched his head and looked at me. 'We measured it all correctly, did we not, Nathan?' he said.

'We did,' I said.

Then Williams said: 'Sir, we have forgotten to take something into account in our measurements.'

'Oh, and what's that?' asked Aldo.

'The veranda, sir.'

'The veranda?'

'Yes, sir. The kitchen runs beneath the veranda. That's at least an extra four paces.'

'By Jove!' said Aldo, his face brightening. 'Another four paces! Take us to the veranda, Williams. At the double, if you please.'

We didn't even stop to put on our coats. Aldo bundled us out into the chilly outdoors, and made us watch as he paced out the veranda, not once but twice. The veranda measured six paces from the outer wall to the stone balustrade. 'Are you sure the kitchen comes out to here?' he said to Williams.

'Yes, sir,' he said. 'I've been living here since 1859, as footman then butler to Mr Genton, the mistress's father. I've seen plenty of work done on the place in that time. There was subsidence at the front here about ten years ago, when the roots of that old tree were thought to be damaging the foundations.' He gestured to the dead tree on the lawn. 'They killed the tree with poison, but the master didn't want it chopped down, so there it remains. Then the workmen came and dug up the lawn below where we're standing. I remember seeing the back wall of the kitchen exposed. That's how I know the kitchen runs beneath the veranda.'

Aldo looked at Lily and then at me. 'Six extra paces,' he said. 'How do you explain that?'

'Let's go back inside,' Lily shivered. 'I can't think out here.'

We decided to pace it all out again, just to be sure. This time we measured the ground floor first, and then the basement. The result was the same: thirty-eight paces upstairs, and thirty-two paces downstairs. Then we stood in Williams' office and tried to puzzle the thing out.

'Somewhere down here, we've lost six paces,' I said.

'Have we allowed for wall thicknesses?' asked Lily.

'There are three rooms downstairs, four upstairs,' I counted, 'if we include the veranda. But a wall is only about a foot thick – not nearly enough to explain the difference.'

Aldo tapped the southern wall of the office with his knuckle. 'How thick is this wall, Williams?'

'I've no idea, sir.'

'This is the only wall down here where the thickness can't be verified,' Aldo pointed out. 'The other wall has a doorway in it. I'll wager this is where we'll find the missing six paces.'

'But why the devil would they build such a thick wall?' I asked.

Aldo didn't reply – he only pointed to the ceiling. 'What is directly above here, Williams?'

'The library, sir.'

'What part of the library?'

'The hearth, I think.'

'The hearth!' I cried. 'Where the ghost disappeared!'

Aldo tapped the wall again. 'Within these walls,' he muttered. 'John Rathborn said, "I will make arrangements for you to live *within these walls*."'

CHAPTER

10

e returned to the library, and examined the hearth. 'Do you notice anything unusual about the brickwork at the back here?' Aldo asked.

I studied it. 'The bricks are new and red,' I observed. 'There are none of the scorch marks you'd expect to see in a working fireplace.'

Aldo turned to Williams. 'Have you had many fires in this room?' he asked him.

'Mr Genton only used the library occasionally, owing to its gloominess,' responded Williams, 'while Mr John Rathborn used it a great deal for the very same reason. I would say there have been a fair few fires built here, and most of them in the past two years.' His face creased in thought. 'I suppose the last fire we had in here was in April.'

'And has any renovation been done to the hearth since then?'

'None that I know of, sir.'

'So how do you explain the clean appearance of the bricks?' he asked. 'They look to me as if they were laid last week.'

The elderly butler reached for a pair of eyeglasses and pushed them up his nose. He shambled closer and peered at the brickwork at the rear of the hearth. 'I agree with you, sir,' he said after a moment. 'And I can't explain it.'

Aldo stepped back from the fireplace and looked at Lily and me. 'What say you, colleagues?' he asked.

'Those bricks will have to come down,' I said.

'We should speak to our hosts,' said Lily.

In the hallway, we ran into father and Daniel, just returned from the stables. Father was smiling. 'Johnson thinks it will be safe to go back to London on horseback,' he said. 'I will set off after lunch, with James. Daniel will ride with us. So, tell me, you three: how are your investigations going? Have you discovered the identity of Nathan's ghost?'

'We've made a number of important discoveries this morning,' I said.

'We'd like to go through them with both of you and Mrs Rathborn, if you have time,' added Lily.

'Of course,' said Father.

Mrs Rathborn emerged from the back parlour, a magazine in her hand. 'Did I hear talk of discoveries?' she asked.

Daniel nodded. 'You heard correctly, mother. Shall we all go into the drawing room?'

Everyone took a seat while Aldo pounded the carpet, assembling his thoughts. He began his report with the discovery of the diary. He was careful to point out that Sara Teltree had not read a word of it, and he was purposely vague about most of its contents. 'I will not bore you with the details,' he said. 'You may read it for yourselves, if you wish. But there are a few aspects that I would like to make known to you, as they are germane to our investigation. These are sensitive matters, regarding the private lives of the members of this household.' His gaze fell on Daniel and Mrs Rathborn. 'If either of you wish me to stop right there, I shall.'

'I'm sorry, Aldo,' said Daniel, 'but fascinating as all this below-stairs gossip is, I cannot for the life of me see what it has to do with your enquiry.'

'It has everything to do with the enquiry,' replied Aldo. 'In fact, I would go so far as to say that your permission for me to talk openly about these matters is essential to the progress of our investigation.'

'I knew about Polly and John,' said Mrs Rathborn quietly, her face grey and expressionless. 'I assume that is what you were about to reveal, Aldo.'

Aldo nodded.

Mrs Rathborn turned to me. 'I'm sorry, Nathan, for lying to you the other night. I told you that Richard Culpin had fathered Polly's child. I knew this was not the case. I had hoped that none of this... unpleasantness would need to become known. I never dreamed, when I asked you three to help with some bumps in the night, that it would lead to the unveiling of this tawdry episode. But there you are. It's embarrassing, but I suppose we need to confront it.'

'Mother, we don't need to confront anything,' said Daniel urgently. 'This is a private family matter. It has nothing to do with these people.'

Mrs Rathborn grasped her son's arm and gently squeezed it. 'I *want* to talk about it.' Her eyes became clouded, as though turned back on the past. 'One morning,' she said, 'twelve months ago, Daniel informed me that John was having an affair with the maid, Polly O'Brien. He told me the girl was pregnant – I had to assume the child was John's. I asked Mrs Haverhill to dismiss Polly that same day, and I made John swear that he would have nothing more to do with the girl or her child. It wasn't that I was jealous. If I must own the truth, my husband and I grew apart during the long course of our marriage. By that time, he was no more than a friend to me. What he did in his private life was of no interest to me, so long as it remained private. But getting a maid pregnant was overstepping the mark, as far as I was concerned. It risked scandal, and that was not something I could tolerate. John told me he had arranged for the girl to go and live with Richard Culpin. I don't know the details of the agreement he made with Mr Culpin, but John told me that it was his hope that the man would marry Polly before the baby was born and that they would raise the child as their own. That is all I know about the matter. Is this consistent with what you read in the diary?'

This was, of course, quite different from Polly's version of events. For one thing, there was no mention of Daniel's sordid role in bringing the affair to light. And second, according to the diary, Mrs Rathborn had *not* forbidden her husband from seeing Polly again. In fact, she had agreed to divorce him, so long as the house could remain in her hands.

Aldo looked uncomfortable. 'So you never agreed to a divorce?' he said.

'Why of course not!' replied Mrs Rathborn, looking quite horrified. 'What an idea! As if John would ever have considered giving up all this, and his place in society, for a servant girl.'

'The idea was never even discussed?'

'Of course not! Why do you ask? Is that what the girl's written in her diary?'

'The girl may have fantasised that part of it,' broke in Lily. 'She certainly appeared to be in a very agitated state, to judge from her handwriting.'

'She has a powerful imagination, I will grant her that,' said Mrs Rathborn.

'Whatever our speculations about Polly O'Brien's state of mind,' said Aldo, 'I'm afraid the evidence still suggests that your late husband lied to you, Mrs Rathborn. He did *not* hope that Culpin would marry Polly, because he made plans to move Polly back *here*. And I have strong reason to believe that those plans were carried out.'

Mrs Rathborn's eyes opened wide with shock. Her son leapt to his feet, his cheeks aflame. 'By all the gods, now I really have heard enough!' he bellowed. 'How dare you stand there and slander my father! Are you asking us to believe the preposterous scribblings of some harlot over the word of my own flesh and blood? Withdraw that statement now, sir, or I must ask you to leave this house!'

Aldo merely smiled. 'I will not withdraw the statement, because I believe it to be true.'

'Aldo, I sincerely hope you have more evidence to support this than the diary of a housemaid,' said Father, a touch anxiously.

'I do,' said Aldo.

Daniel was still on his feet and looked ready to punch Aldo if he uttered a further syllable he didn't agree with. It was a look I remembered seeing on the face of a boy named Giles Sinclair at St Paul's School when he was enraged by one of my brother's too-clever remarks. The look was always a prelude to violence, first from him and then from me, as I leapt to Aldo's defence. I felt the old hackles rising now, but I wasn't too concerned – Daniel Rathborn was more bark than bite. 'Well?' he said. 'Are you going to tell us what this evidence is?'

So Aldo did. He quoted the enigmatic words that Polly recorded John Rathborn as telling her, and he explained how that had set him wondering about whether there might be a secret room somewhere in the house. He spoke of the missing six paces in the basement and how we had managed to locate this to a gap that existed between the butler's office and the scullery. Finally, he recounted our examination of the library fireplace and its mysteriously new-looking brickwork. 'This fireplace,' he concluded, 'lies directly above that inexplicable gap in the basement, and it also happens to be the same hearth into which Nathan saw a ghost disappear – a ghost that was identified by Alice Birch as looking very much like Polly.'

Daniel was thrown into temporary silence by these disclosures, but he soon recovered his voice. 'Are you really suggesting,' he said contemptuously, 'that the girl was living in the basement without the knowledge of anyone in this house? I assume you don't believe she's still living there now?'

'I would think not,' said Aldo. 'If we are to believe Nathan's account of the ghost, her point of access to the secret room was most likely the library fireplace – until this was bricked up. No person could possibly be living down there still, as it is completely closed in, upstairs and downstairs.'

I shivered a little as I heard Aldo say this, recalling the girl with the white face, and her baby. Had they died down there? The thought was too hideous to contemplate.

'Did either of you order any recent renovations to the fireplace in question?' asked Father, addressing Daniel and Mrs Rathborn.

'Absolutely not,' said Daniel.

'No, Mr Carter, this is all news to me,' said Mrs Rathborn. 'I can only imagine that if there was any work done on it, it would have been arranged by… well, by John.'

A silence descended as I, and perhaps everyone else, contemplated the implications of her words. Had John Rathborn literally buried his problem?

'There's one way of testing all this, of course,' said Father. 'If Mrs Rathborn and Daniel are amenable to the idea, we could simply knock through the brickwork at the back of the fireplace. Supposing Aldo is right, we should find a door there. If not, then –'

'Then I will immediately resign from the case, and leave you good people in peace,' finished Aldo.

'I will not stand for any desecration of this house,' said Daniel.

'It's hardly a desecration, young man,' said Father genially. 'We're merely talking about the removal of a few bricks. And if there's nothing there, we'll put them back again. It won't cost you or your mother a penny. I'll gladly cover all the expenses. It'll be well worth the cost, if only to restore our collective peace of mind. What do you say, Mrs Rathborn?'

'I think we should do it,' she said quietly.

A builder named Elwood Gunn was summoned from the village, and after lunch we all gathered in the library to watch him set to work. First he removed the grate, then used a hammer and chisel to start chipping away the cement that surrounded the central bricks. He worked slowly and carefully, under orders from Daniel to minimise the damage and, if possible, to leave the bricks intact, so they could be reused. After about a quarter of an hour, Mr Gunn was able to remove the first brick. All was shadow at first, but when a second brick was removed a few minutes later, we began to discern something of what lay behind.

'I fail to see your door, Aldo,' sneered Daniel. 'It looks like more bricks to me!'

No one could dispute this observation. As the wall was gradually dismantled, we saw before us nothing more exciting than the dirty grey-brown brickwork of the original hearth.

'It looks as though you've wasted your money, Mr Carter,' said Daniel, as the last few bricks were removed and an ordinary, undistinguished wall lay exposed. 'A perfectly fine piece of brickwork has been demolished to satisfy the vanity of your son.'

'Not so fine, if I may make so bold, sir,' said Mr Gunn. 'Those bricks were not well laid, and the cement was poorly applied. When I put them back for you, sir, I shall make a far better job of it. Who, may I ask, did this work for you?'

'That is as much a mystery, Mr Gunn, as everything else about this business,' said Mrs Rathborn. 'We don't know who commissioned the work, who carried it out, nor why it was done. For my part I cannot see the gain in covering one wall with another inferior one.'

Aldo was crouching in the hearth, peering closely at the exposed wall. He kicked aside some rubble, and got to his knees. Placing his hands on the wall's surface, he pushed. Nothing happened. He ran his left hand over the surface, no doubt searching for a hidden knob or handle, but found nothing. Then he seemed to become intrigued by something at the bottom of the wall where it met the floor.

'What have you seen, Aldo?' I asked.

He did not reply, but turned his gaze to the top of the wall, near the entrance to the chimney, and ran his fingers along something there. 'Mr Gunn,' he called. 'Is there any reason why we should find these grooves here and here?' He indicated a pair of almost invisible parallel channels running along the top and bottom of the wall.

Gunn peered close. 'None that I can think of, sir' he muttered. 'Unless this wall was designed to be removed.'

Aldo pushed at it again, this time assisted by Gunn, but the wall remained as solid and fixed as ever.

They sat back on their haunches, seemingly baffled. So I stepped into the gap between them and tried giving it an experimental push. Then another idea came to me. I inserted my fingertips into a shallow gap between two bricks and tried to push sideways from left to right. There was a deep grumbling sound, like the reluctant shifting of a long-embedded stone, and I thought I detected a slight movement. I placed the fingertips of my other hand in another gap and pushed with both hands. This time, amid more grinding, the wall definitely shifted an inch or more, revealing a thin strip of the deepest black on the far left. 'Help me,' I said, and Aldo and Gunn lent their hands to the cause. With a powerful jolt, the wall rolled all the way open, and we found ourselves staring into a hollow space, some four feet deep. It appeared to be part of a circular, brick-lined shaft. A set of spiral steps led downwards from the back of the fireplace. The brickwork and the stone steps looked old – as old as the house itself – and the thought struck me, as it must have simultaneously struck Mrs Rathborn, that this secret space had been here for a very long time – it had been here even as she, as a young girl, had played her innocent games in this room. Surprise was evident on the faces of everyone present, especially Daniel and Lily.

Aldo smiled at me. 'Good work, brother.' He cocked an eyebrow at Daniel. 'Do you still wish to attribute this investigation to my vanity, sir?' he demanded.

Daniel recovered his poise and looked down his nose at him. 'Your instincts have proved right on this occasion,' he conceded. 'You appear to have uncovered a priest-hole of some description. But I remain unconvinced that any person recently alive could have dwelt down there.'

'Light me a candle,' said Aldo, his foot already on the first step of the staircase, 'and I'll see if I can find you proof.'

'Oh, do take care, Aldo!' cried Mrs Rathborn. 'It looks very old and unsafe, and I dread to think what you might find at the bottom of those steps!' She didn't say any more, and didn't need to. I suspected she shared my own fears in that regard.

Father placed a reassuring hand on Mrs Rathborn's arm, as Williams, who had earlier limped into the room to see what all the clamour was about, handed Aldo a lit candle.

'Brother,' Aldo said, turning to me. 'Follow me down. I need you with me as a witness.' Again, there was no need to spell out his thinking. As the sole witness to the ghost, I was needed there to recognise it if the thing reappeared.

I almost turned him down. Ashamed as I am to admit it, such a fear had laid hold of me at the sight of those ancient steps spiralling into the gloom, that I became quite immobilised. If I could have spoken, I would probably have asked to be excused.

If I could have moved, it would have been to run as far away as possible. Into my thoughts came the ice-white maiden. I could see her as clearly as the people standing before me now. Her eyes stared through me, and then I watched her disappear into the wall where Aldo now stood. She must have descended those steps. She would be waiting for us at the bottom.

Aldo, reading my thoughts, said softly: 'Banish those fears, Nathan. I shall go first and if this candle fails to reflect in the eyes of any person we meet, I shall be the first to see it.'

His words stirred me from my paralysis and I began to feel very foolish. I seized the candle from him. 'I shall lead the way,' I said, and Aldo shrugged and stood aside to let me pass.

Slowly, with my hands gripping the cold stone of the central column for balance, I descended the steps. With every narrow downward tread taking me deeper into the shadows, the knot inside my stomach tightened. I kept anticipating a movement – the sudden appearance of a foot or a leg, or worse, a face. I won't tell you what I imagined on that short descent. Even now, I don't know how I managed to keep placing one foot after the other, but I did, and at the bottom I came up against a wooden door.

'This must be the basement,' whispered Aldo, close behind and above me. He tapped the rear of the stairwell. 'Beyond here is the scullery. Now open the door, Nathan.'

I found I could not do it. My left hand, holding the candle, was shaking, casting hulking, juddering shadows on the walls and door. My right hand was glued to my side, nails digging into my palm.

'It's only a door,' said Aldo gently. 'And behind it is a room. Only a room.'

My right hand flexed and my damp fingers found the door handle – a cold black metal ring. From somewhere came the will and strength to twist it, and we heard the sound of a latch rising. Closing my eyes, I pushed at the handle and heard a quiet creak as the door opened.

My nostrils were immediately assailed by the sweet stench of decay. I felt Aldo push past me into the room, as I stood there in the doorway, eyes still tightly shut. I waited for a cry or exclamation, but he made no sound.

'What is it, Aldo? What can you see?'

'Come closer with your light, brother. Stop dithering over there by the door.'

Relieved he hadn't been struck dumb or insane, I opened my eyes and fully entered the room. The candlelight fell on a simple room furnished with a single bed, a cot, a chest and a wardrobe. Two dishes of decayed food lay on the floor by the bed: one almost eaten, the other hardly touched.

However, very few of these details registered until some while later, as our immediate attention was riveted by the sight on the bed. Curled up there on the counterpane were the bodies of a woman and a baby. The infant was scarcely visible, being wrapped up and held close to the woman's chest, yet I could not mistake the awful sight of a tiny, shrivelled, brown hand resting on the woman's upper arm. The skin of the woman's face had the quality of dried leather – dark and shiny, and stretched tightly over the bones of her skull, cheek and jaw. Her head seemed shrunken, and her teeth were prominent between thin, brown lips. Nausea filled me as recognition dawned: the maid's clothing, the vivid red hair, even the shape of the cheekbones – here lay the beauty I had witnessed the night before, made hideous by the corrupting influence of death.

Part 2

CHAPTER

11

n Tuesday 21 November, one week after our departure from Gravewood Hall, we attended the inquest into Richard Culpin's death at Hertford Coroner's Court. I was tense during the journey there. Despite all the reassurances I had received from Daniel Rathborn and Father, I could not help fearing that the officials might take a different view of the affair. The court was packed with spectators when we arrived, which did not improve my state of mind. However, once in the witness stand, answering questions, I grew in confidence, and this only increased as I heard what the other witnesses had to say. Inspector Simmons, Aldo, Father, Mrs Rathborn and several members

of the household staff all gave evidence. After that we heard from half a dozen witnesses from Winterby village, who were all, to a man or woman, scathing of Culpin's character. It seemed the fellow did not have many friends – in death or in life. After listening to all this, the jury of eight local men had no hesitation in returning a verdict of 'death by misadventure'. Inspector Simmons then confirmed that he would not be pursuing the case. Of course, this came as a great relief to me.

We were required to be in the Coroner's Court again the following morning for the inquest into the deaths of Polly and her son, James O'Brien. Mrs Rathborn invited us to stay the night at Gravewood, but Father graciously declined, having already booked us rooms at an inn in town. I'm sure these could have been cancelled if Father had been so inclined, but he probably found the idea of staying at Gravewood Hall inappropriate, given the circumstances, and I fully agreed with him.

The following morning, we reconvened at the Coroner's Court. Again, it was standing room only in the courtroom, and many of the spectators seemed to be journalists eager for a scoop. The grisly 'buried alive' story had captured the public imagination – particularly so because the victims were a mother and baby. It dominated that morning's *Hertfordshire Mercury* and had even made the front pages of several London papers. Aldo and I were the first witnesses to be called. The coroner asked us, in turn, to give our account of what we had seen on entering the hidden room. I offered as objective a description as I could, though my memory of that experience was so overlaid with nausea and fear that I found it hard to speak of it coherently.

After us, the court heard the testimony of a London-based pathologist by the name of Mr Thomas Clover, who had examined the bodies of mother and child, as well as the remains of the food found near them. He reported that the bodies had 'scarcely decomposed', owing to the cool, dry conditions in the basement room, and this made establishing the date of death quite a challenge. However, it was his opinion that mother and child had died between three and five weeks before the date of their discovery; in other words, between the tenth and the twenty-fourth of October. When asked about probable cause of death, he stated (to gasps of shock in the courtroom) that he had found traces of rat poison in the stomach of the baby, as well as in the food on the plates, but none in the stomach of the mother. It was his conclusion that the baby had died from ingesting the strychnine in the rat poison, but that the mother had died more gradually, probably from dehydration, over a period of days. He had also performed a chemical analysis on the proprietary brand of rat poison kept in the basement storeroom at Gravewood Hall, and found that it was a perfect match to the traces found in the food and in the baby's stomach.

Inspector Simmons, who was also in charge of this case, then delivered his own findings. He showed, with the help of photographs, that there were scratch marks and other signs of recent damage to the rear of the secret door – that is, the moveable brick wall that lay behind the more recently constructed one. This led him to conclude that Polly O'Brien had attempted to escape from the subterranean room, but had failed because the secret door – her usual means of access – had become jammed, probably due to the fact that a second brick wall had been laid immediately in front of it.

Mrs Haverhill took the stand to confirm that the body of the woman, so far as she could tell, as the face was 'gruesomely altered', belonged to the former housemaid, Polly O'Brien. The coroner asked her if she had any knowledge of the secret room or of Polly's residence there. To both queries she indignantly replied in the negative. As to the rat poison, she said that rats were a constant problem in the basement areas of the house, and she had purchased a new tin as recently as September (she couldn't remember the date) from the apothecary in Winterby village.

Next into the witness box was Alice Birch, dressed in her Sunday best for her day in the spotlight. She told the court that she had known Polly as a friend, but had not seen her since June. In the weeks following Polly's disappearance, Alice had asked after her among mutual acquaintances in the village, including Richard Culpin, but neither he nor anyone else could say where she had gone. Polly had often spoken of returning to London, and Alice had assumed that she had gone off to pursue a new life in the city.

Did Alice know of the secret room before its recent discovery? Not at all. Did she have any theories as to why Polly O'Brien had apparently been dwelling in secret in the basement of Gravewood Hall for the four months between June and October this year? Alice said she had been deeply shocked and distressed to learn that her friend had been living among them for all those weeks without their knowledge. She said that the staff were all still very upset about it, especially considering the fate of that poor baby, and it would be a while before they could feel comfortable again about living and working in that house. She said she couldn't for the life of her understand how a girl like Polly could have coped with that kind of imprisonment or why she would ever have agreed to it.

One by one, the other members of staff were called to the stand and asked about Polly and the secret room. Those who had known her spoke of their liking for the girl and all expressed shock and sadness at her apparent incarceration and death in their midst. Mrs Partridge, the cook, said she had noticed some food going missing over the summer and autumn and had assumed it was one of the servants, but she hadn't reported it, as the amounts were quite small. The coroner asked Mr Williams, the butler, whether he had ordered, supervised or witnessed any renovations to the library fireplace over the past year. The elderly butler said he had been wracking his memory all week on this point, but had to confess that he had no memory of anything concerning that fireplace. 'The library,' he said, 'was used almost exclusively by Mr John until his death. It was cleaned once a week by one of the housemaids, and that was the only time anyone else went in there. I can only think that Mr John laid those bricks himself, or else directly contracted an outside person to do it. But why the master should wish to entomb that poor girl and her baby, I cannot think. He was always so kind to me, I just cannot imagine –' At this point, the coroner reminded the witness that the purpose of an inquest was to establish how a death came about, not to apportion guilt or attribute blame.

After a recess for lunch, Mrs Rathborn took the stand, causing a small flurry of excitement around the court. I felt great sympathy for the lady, as I surveyed the eager faces of the scribes in the front row of the spectators' seats, licking their pencils and waiting for her to speak. She was a proud woman, and it must have been difficult for her to hold forth publicly on such matters, yet she did not hesitate to state the truth as she knew it. She spoke frankly about her late husband's affair with Polly, the girl's pregnancy and her decision to dismiss her. She said she had asked her husband not to see Polly again and had believed him when he said he wouldn't. But, in the light of the discovery in the basement, she had been forced reluctantly to accept that he had lied to her. 'He must have somehow discovered this room under the library,' she told the court, '– a room he then quietly turned into a hidey-hole for his mistress. I suppose he was working on that little project all through the early part of this year, unbeknownst to me or anyone else.' She sighed and shook her head. 'The cruelty of keeping a woman and her infant son in that cramped little space for all those months is something that I will never be able to understand or forgive him for. I can only speculate on what promises he made to her, or else why would the girl ever have agreed to exist in such wretched confinement?'

Daniel Rathborn had been unable to attend the Coroner's Court, as he was involved (in a professional capacity) in another court case in London. In his written statement, which was read out to the court, he denied any knowledge of the secret room or of Polly's habitation there. And there, or thereabouts, the testimony came to an end. The coroner, to no one's surprise, returned a verdict of 'unlawful killing', and it was then left to Inspector Simmons and the Hertfordshire Constabulary to decide how to proceed.

For my part, I could not understand why John Rathborn would choose to kill Polly and little Jimmy. This was a man, after all, who had gone to such unusual lengths to take his mistress and son back into his home. For four months he had lived a precarious double life, caring for his basement family while continuing to present a normal face to the outside world. Why, after such efforts, would he poison his new family and bury them alive?

I tried to imagine what their lives had been like during those summer and autumn months. He had probably visited her and the child regularly, taking them food he had pilfered from the pantry. Perhaps he had allowed her to venture out from time to time and they had shared nocturnal meals in the servants' hall. These were the occasions that Polly must have lived for. She would have fantasised that they were already married, sharing a modest house somewhere in the suburbs of London, while believing his tender reassurances that her long-wished-for future was imminent. And then, one October night, John Rathborn had put rat poison into two plates of chicken stew and taken it downstairs to his mistress and son. After kissing them both goodbye, he had returned to the library and ordered someone to brick up the fireplace.

What could have goaded him to such a change of heart? Had Polly become threatening? Had she become deranged? Even then, a man so driven by love would surely have preferred exposure and ruin to cold-blooded murder. Of course, if John Rathborn *had* killed Polly and little James, he would have had to do so before his own death on the fifteenth of October. The pathologist had given the earliest likely date of Polly and James's death as the tenth of October. Something awful must have happened to the man during that five-day period – some fit of frenzy. It was a mercy, in some ways, that he did not have to live for too long with the guilt and sorrow at what he had done.

ne evening, a few days after the second inquest, Lily, Aldo and I were relaxing in the parlour at home, each of us absorbed in our own activities. Aldo was in his favourite armchair, by the window, sketching a still life consisting of a table lamp and a small pile of books. His lean, unshaven face, beneath a mop of tousled black hair, was utterly preoccupied in the task. I was seated close to the fire, playing solitaire, while Lily was on the sofa, reading a book.

Suddenly, she looked up. 'This is interesting,' she remarked.

'What is?' I asked.

'I'm reading an account of the trial of William Palmer.'

'The Staffordshire poisoner?' frowned Aldo, still sketching.

'The very same.'

'Well, what of it?'

'He used strychnine,' said Lily, 'the active ingredient in the rat poison that killed Polly O'Brien's baby.'

We both turned to look at her.

'Palmer was hanged a quarter of a century ago,' Aldo pointed out. 'You can't possibly suspect him of this one.'

'No, silly, I'm only reading about his trial because I wanted to find out more about this poison. Anyway, it says here that the symptoms of strychnine poisoning are very similar to those of tetanus.'

'Isn't that what John Rathborn died from?' I asked.

'Exactly!' said Lily, and I suddenly saw what she was driving at. 'Listen to this,' she said. 'Here's the testimony of Dr Robert Todd, an expert witness at the trial: "I have no doubt the peculiar irritation of the nerves in tetanus is identical with the peculiar irritation of the nerves in strychnine poisoning." And another witness, Professor Robert Christison, agrees that there is very little difference in the symptoms between the two, only that tetanus advances more slowly than strychnine poisoning.

But John Rathborn died quickly, didn't he? I understood he took ill on the evening of the fifteenth of October, and then died in the early hours of the sixteenth. Well, that sounds a lot more like strychnine than tetanus to me. Of course, I'm no physician, but it's just possible the doctor was a little hasty in his diagnosis that night.'

'Do you think Inspector Simmons is aware of this?' I asked.

'I'm sure he isn't,' said Aldo. 'No one has thought to link the death of John Rathborn to those of Polly and little James – no one until Lily, that is.'

'This could change everything,' I said. 'We should go to the police.'

'Wait!' said Lily. 'Let's think this through. What are you saying, Nathan?'

I looked at her. At first she had been flushed with the excitement of discovery, but now she looked disturbed at its implications. 'Of course it's possible that John Rathborn killed his belowstairs family, and then himself,' she muttered.

'Or that a third party found out about the affair and decided to kill all three,' I said.

'A third party?' Again she looked worried.

'Well let's look at potential suspects,' I said. 'It could have been Daniel Rathborn. Or...' I hesitated as the ramifications struck me as well. I had been about to say Mrs Rathborn, but even thinking it felt like a betrayal after the support and friendship she had shown me.

This was no game we were playing. The decision we took now could affect the lives of people we knew and cared about.

'I know that Nathan has a soft spot for Mrs Rathborn,' smiled Aldo, 'and you, Lily, are somewhat partial to her son. But both of you will have to put your personal feelings aside for the sake of justice. Let's say we write to Simmons tomorrow and he takes us up on our hunch and decides to exhume John Rathborn's body. And let's say a post-mortem reveals signs of strychnine poisoning. Then I'm afraid your two friends are likely to become suspects in a triple murder enquiry. After all, they both had the means and the motive. The rat poison was there, in the house. Either of them might have spied John Rathborn and Polly on one of their nightly trysts. Mrs Rathborn would have felt angered and betrayed. As for Daniel, we've heard from several sources about his fights with his father and his desperation to inherit the business.'

'I don't believe for one minute that Daniel killed his father to inherit the business,' said Lily. 'But even if he did, why would he also want to kill Polly and her baby?'

'Who knows?' shrugged Aldo 'He may have still been angry with her for rejecting him. Or maybe she witnessed the murder of his father, and she had to be silenced.'

We sat there, the three of us, for some while afterwards, meditating on these possibilities. In my opinion, and without allowing personal feelings to enter into it, Daniel Rathborn was a far more plausible suspect than his mother. By her own admission, she had not been in love with her husband for a very long time, so jealousy could not have been a motive. Her only concern had been the avoidance of scandal, and poisoning three people seemed like a tremendous risk to take for someone who simply wanted a quiet life. What if the doctor had correctly diagnosed poisoning rather than tetanus? What if Polly had somehow made her presence known before she had died? It may have been my 'soft spot' as Aldo had termed it, but I simply could not imagine Mrs Rathborn as the murderer.

The following morning, we showed Father the relevant passages in Lily's book. He became very grave and silent. Then he took up his pen and wrote a letter, as follows:

Inspector Jonah Simmons
Hertfordshire Constabulary
Bale Road , Hertford

24 November 1882

Dear Inspector,

I am writing to you in connection with the O'Brien
case, which I understand you are presently
investigating. You are no doubt aware that the
recent death of Mr John Rathborn, former employer
of Miss Polly O'Brien, was officially ascribed to
tetanus. With this in mind, it may interest you to
consult the transcripts of the trial, in 1856, of
the murderer Mr William Palmer, in particular the
expert testimony detailing the similarities between
the symptoms of tetanus and those of strychnine
poisoning. (This item, I should point out, was
brought to my attention by my niece, Miss Lily
Morelle.) I leave it entirely to your discretion as to
whether you wish to pursue such a line of enquiry,
and will not presume to say any more on the matter.

Yours, etc.,
Samuel Carter

Seven days later, my father received the following
response, which he read out to the three of us:

Samuel Carter, Esq.
14 Waverley Terrace
St John's Wood
London

1 December 1882

Sir, I am most indebted to you for your letter of
24th November, drawing my attention to the
undoubted correspondence between the physical
symptoms of tetanus and strychnine poisoning.
I have since studied the transcripts of the Palmer
trial in detail and consulted with Dr Brett, who
attended Mr Rathborn in his final hours and was
responsible for drawing up the death certificate.
Dr Brett has told me that he wishes to stand by
his original verdict that Mr Rathborn was a
victim of tetanus. However, after a further
conversation with the pathologist Mr Clover, I
decided, last Tuesday, to order the exhumation of
Mr Rathborn's body.
Mr Clover's post-mortem report, received earlier
this day, confirms the suspicions that evidently
motivated your letter. Traces of rat poison were
found in the stomach contents of Mr John
Rathborn, and these are a perfect match to the
samples found in the stomach of James O'Brien
and in the plates of food. Furthermore, Mr Clover

*could find no evidence of a scar or wound to the
skin of the deceased that might have provided a
means of entry for the tetanus infection. On this
basis, he has respectfully requested a revision to the
death certificate to the effect that Mr John
Rathborn died of strychnine poisoning.*

*My thanks again to you, sir, and to your sharp-
eyed niece. Your insight has led to an important
breakthrough in the case. However, I would urge
you to keep these findings to yourself, at least until
tomorrow, when an announcement will appear in
the local and national press.*

*I remain, Sir, your obedient servant,
Jonah Simmons (Inspector)*

The following morning, we were eating breakfast
when Graves came in and handed Father his copy
of *The Times*. Lily and I immediately clustered
around the back of Father's chair, while Aldo
calmly got on with his boiled egg.

Lily soon located a small piece near the bottom
of page one, headlined 'Breakthrough in
O'Brien case'. It reported on the exhumation and
the revised cause of death, and we were also startled
to read, near the end of the article, that Mr Daniel
Rathborn had been asked to assist the police with
their enquiries.

Lily clutched her face in her hands. 'Oh, what have I done?' she cried. 'Uncle, you must write to him at once. I want to know what has happened.'

'Can I finish my breakfast first, Lily?' chuckled Father. And then he became serious. 'You knew the possible consequences, my dear, when you showed me those trial transcripts. And you knew I had no choice but to write to the inspector. I loved John Rathborn, whatever he may or may not have done towards the end of his life, and I want to see justice served – for him, and for Polly and little James. Whatever happens in the future, you were right to show me those transcripts. And now we must place our trust in the legal process, and whatever will be will be.'

'But Daniel's fights with his father were common knowledge,' said Lily. 'The police will surely seize on that, not to mention the lies that Polly wrote about him in her diary.'

'And what "lies" are you referring to?' asked Father.

'She claimed that he assaulted her in his bedroom after he discovered her with his father,' said Lily. 'He threatened her with dismissal unless she offered similar favours to him, or so she says.'

'I see,' frowned Father.

'I very much doubt that diary still exists,' said Aldo between bites of his toast. 'Nathan, you handed it to Daniel before our departure, am I right?'

I nodded.

'Then no doubt the first thing he did, after giving it a quick read-through, was to cast it on the fire.'

'Knowing young Daniel as I do, I would agree with you there, Aldo,' said Father. 'But let us not prejudge the man. Even if he *did* destroy the diary, he may only have been acting to preserve his reputation as a gentleman. It does not make him a murderer. And as for his quarrels with his father, you may take comfort, Lily, that these might arouse suspicion, but they are not in themselves enough to convict him. The police would have to find something a lot more conclusive before Daniel Rathborn finds himself before the hangman.'

'Uncle!' admonished Lily. 'How can I take any comfort when you put it that way? Now, I can see no more breakfast on your plate nor tea in your cup, so I must ask, what can possibly delay you from going this minute to your study to write to Mr Rathborn?'

Under much token protest, Father allowed himself to be dragged to his study. The letter he eventually produced, to Lily's disappointment, did not refer directly to recent developments in the O'Brien saga, but merely expressed his good wishes and offered his services as a friend. 'This is vague in the extreme,' she said when she'd read it. 'He will wonder why you have written to him at all.'

Father merely sighed. 'I have done my best, dear.'

'We all do our best, Father,' remarked Aldo. 'But that is never a guarantee that it will please Lily.'

Later that morning, Father wrote another letter, this time to Mrs Rathborn, but refrained from disclosing its contents to us.

Three days later, we were again seated at the breakfast table when Graves brought Father a letter with a Hertfordshire postmark.

'Open it, quickly,' gasped Lily. 'It must be from Mr Rathborn.'

But the letter turned out to be from his mother. Father read it to us:

4 December 1882

Dear Mr Carter,

Thank you so much for your recent letter. It is a great comfort during this time of turmoil to know that I can count on your friendship. As you have no doubt read, Daniel has been questioned by the police. They have not, as yet, charged him with any crime, but we are living in a constant state of anxiety and dread. The noises continue at night, and I have found sleeping almost impossible of late.

I do so miss your family's cheerful presence here
at Gravewood, which has become a noticeably
colder place since your departure, despite the
improved weather. The servants have been quiet
and uneasy since the discovery of the hidden room
and its dreadful secret, and they move about the
house like fearful mice (it almost seems at times as
though I, like the poor O'Brien girl, am living
alone here, forgotten by the world).

I am sorry, Mr Carter. I know you are a busy
man and I am making you impatient with my
self-indulgent talk. So I will come straight to the
point. I should like to invite you and your family
for a return visit to Gravewood Hall. If you are
free this coming Wednesday (6 December), we
would be delighted to welcome you then. I can guess
what you are thinking. Daniel was not always the
most charming of hosts during your recent visit,
but I assure you he has become a much quieter
and, in his own way, more amenable person in the
past two weeks. I won't say he will ever exhibit
the warmth and generosity of spirit of his father,
but I have nonetheless noticed a change in Daniel
in the wake of recent events. He certainly raised no
objections when I mentioned to him my plan to
invite you here.

Of course, you might have a second objection to a
visit, one which you may never be so blunt as to

speak of to my face, but which could nonetheless
prevent your ever wishing to set foot in this house
again. And to that unmentionable concern, let me
say this: I am convinced of Daniel's innocence of
any charges that he may yet face in relation to the
recent murders. I speak not only as his mother, but
also as a witness to his life and his relationship
with his father. Daniel may have had his differences
with John, but he loved him as any son should. He
was badly affected by John's death, and I feel these
recent revelations have taken a yet deeper toll on
his mental health. To see him now, you would know
immediately that he is one of the victims of these
crimes, not their perpetrator.

The true perpetrator is now dead. You know I
speak of Richard Culpin, for who else could it be?
I am glad, of course, that he is no more, but his
death nonetheless complicates matters, as the
evidence of his crimes has doubtless died with him.
He had the means (we all know how easily he
gained access to the house) and he had the motive:
he hated my husband ever since John evicted him
from this house two years ago, and when the
O'Brien girl left him to go and live with her baby
in the secret room, his hatred of all three grew
into a murderous rage. Even his profession speaks
to his guilt – after all, what more appropriate
means for a bricklayer to conceal his crime than

with that hastily constructed wall in front of the fireplace? I have said all this, at length, and on several occasions, to Inspector Simmons. I will keep saying it until he takes me seriously and desists from treating my son as a suspect in this case.

I apologise once again, Mr Carter. It was not my intention, when I embarked on this letter, that it should become a rant. Please blame it on the aforementioned anxiety. I do hope you will see fit to visit us again soon, but shall not feel in any way slighted if you feel you cannot.

I am, Ever your friend, Mary Rathborn

'We can't go,' I said immediately. 'After what we did, it would be the height of hypocrisy.'

'I disagree,' said Father. 'The Rathborns are our friends, and they need us.'

'But we're the main cause of their distress,' I cried.

'Nonsense,' said Father. 'It was Inspector Simmons's decision to call Daniel in for questioning. We had nothing to do with it.'

'But we knew it would happen. We predicted it.'

'I did what I did for John's sake!' thundered Father, showing a rare flash of temper. 'I'm now going to accept this invitation for the sake of Mary and Daniel. I see no hypocrisy in that, only an act of friendship.'

n a bright, frosty morning, two days later, we made our return journey to Gravewood Hall. Once again, Aldo, Lily, myself and Bonnie shared one of the carriages. Aldo was dressed in a typically absurd patchwork of styles, including olive green trousers and black boots, a purple waistcoat, yellow cravat and his usual shabby velvet coat and battered top hat. He looked like someone from the circus, or from one of London's seedier districts. If Father's budget could have run to it, my brother could certainly have benefited from a personal valet.

Lily was dressed in habitually constrained fashion, with pale, subdued colours, to match her mood. All was rationality and sense, with not a hint of frippery on collar or cuff, nor a single coquettish curl on her forehead. Had she given up on her idea of ensnaring Daniel Rathborn, or was she simply matching herself to her currently penitent disposition?

It was fortunate, perhaps, that we had Bonnie with us, or else the journey might have proceeded largely in silence. Bonnie had read all the latest on the O'Brien case in the gossip sheets, and eagerly filled our ears with it.

'The things I've heard,' she laughed. 'In one paper I read that Mr John was a vampire who couldn't go out in daylight, which was why he had to bring Polly back to live in his house.'

'I hope you're not planning to mention any of this nonsense when we get there,' said Lily sharply.

'Certainly not, my lady.'

'Good, because the staff are disquieted enough as it is.'

'And I shan't mention the other nonsense I read about either.'

'And what nonsense would that be then, Bonnie?' I asked obligingly.

'Well, since you're twisting my arm, sir, I'll have to tell you. Apparently, the reason why the bodies were so thin and well preserved was because he'd eaten all their organs and sucked them dry of blood!'

'Bonnie, that's enough!'

'John Rathborn may not have been a vampire,' said Aldo, 'but he probably suffered from photophobia – an aversion to sunlight. Williams mentioned it, as did Polly in her diary. That was why he gravitated towards the library, the darkest room in the house. And, as Bonnie says, that was most likely why he decided not to keep Polly in a rented cottage in the village, and visit her there. He simply hated going out. In fact, he barely left the house in the last year of his life.'

'That's true, sir,' said Bonnie. 'On our last visit there, Mr Johnson the groom said the master only left the house once a month, to go to the offices of his law firm in London. He carried out all the rest of his business from home, by means of correspondence.'

The winter sun, which had glittered prettily on the holly bushes as we came up the drive, could do little to enliven the rambling bleakness of Gravewood Hall as it came into view. The light fell flat on the grey lawn, as it might on an expanse of cement, and exposed every crack in the surface of the corpse-like tree. The high, sloping roofs with their broken tiles and the peeling paintwork on the shuttered windows looked more sorrowful than sinister, as if the house, having given up its dark secrets, had nothing more to exist for now but a slow decline into ruin.

Mrs Rathborn was in an excited state when we entered the drawing room. She smiled and talked and made a great fuss of us, yet I was worried for her. Her conviviality was of a forced and nervous kind, and her eyes were unnaturally bright. She did not look her usual well-groomed self, and I feared that her mental health, as much as her son's, might have been affected by recent developments.

'Gravewood these past two weeks,' she said, 'has been like a glass-walled prison. I feel the attention of the world on me constantly. We have had news-hounds knocking at the door and creeping through the bushes. And yet, despite all this scrutiny, I have scarcely felt any warmth or human sympathy from anyone. You kind people have been almost alone in offering a friendly ear, a willingness to listen without prejudice to our side of the story. It is astonishing how cold people can be – including people one thought of as friends, but who now only assume the worst. I am afraid there has been more bad news since I wrote to you: Daniel has been ousted from the firm. They have plotted and disguised their little coup in sympathetic language – suggesting he might wish to take some time off until his personal difficulties are resolved – but I'm sure they won't invite him back again, even when his innocence has been proved.'

'How has he taken it?' asked Father.

'He's devastated. Work was his life, as I'm sure you know. He has nothing to occupy himself with now, except the fight to clear his name.'

'We'll be glad to help in any way we can.'

'Thank you so much, Mr Carter,' said Mrs Rathborn, who was by now close to tears.

'Is he here now?' asked Lily

'He went out for his morning ride, dear,' the lady sniffed. 'He should be back before lunch.'

Daniel Rathborn cut a chastened figure at the lunch table. No longer did he eye us in his superior way; in truth, he scarcely looked at us at all, preferring to keep his eyes on his food. Lily did her best to divert him with snippets she had read about in the latest scientific and technical journals:

'I have read, sir,' she said, 'that the physicist Mr Albert Michelson has invented a device for measuring the effect of the Earth's motion on the speed of light.'

'Is that so?' grunted Daniel, picking dolefully at his food.

'And speaking of light,' persevered Lily, 'Mr Thomas Edison of the United States has this very month been illuminating the streets of New York with his new electric light bulb. I so wish I could see such a wonder with my own eyes!'

'I dare say a few of Edison's bulbs wouldn't go amiss in this house,' sighed Daniel. 'They might help the mood.'

'What will help the mood,' said Aldo, 'would be proof of your innocence, and to do that we must find the real culprit.'

Daniel coughed and returned his attention to his food. I wondered whether Aldo had been wise to raise the topic now, but my brother always navigated by his own stars.

'As I said in my letter, the real culprit is Richard Culpin,' Mrs Rathborn pronounced.

'So you say, so you say!' said Aldo. 'And I found your argument most persuasive, Mrs Rathborn. But I also found myself wondering how this man – this great bear of a man – was able not only to gain access to your house, but also to steal the poison, add it to the three plates of food, and then brick up the fireplace – all without anyone noticing. I've no doubt this is what Simmons is wondering, too.'

'You saw for yourself how he was able to get in and out of the house on an almost nightly basis during your last visit here,' replied the lady. 'It seems the man had almost supernatural powers when it came to entering and leaving this property.'

'You forget, Mother, that he lived here for some twenty years before you and Father moved in,' said Daniel. 'He must have been intimately acquainted with every nook and cranny. The place has a secret room. Well, no doubt it has its secret entrances and exits, too.'

'That might deal with Aldo's first point,' said Father. 'But it doesn't explain how he was able to do what he did in the house unobserved.'

'He must have had an accomplice,' said Lily suddenly.

'Voilà!' said Aldo, banging his napkin on the table. 'Lily's absolutely right! He cannot have committed these crimes on his own. How could Culpin have put the poison in Mr Rathborn's meal? Did he creep into the kitchen while Cook was preparing it and spoon in the rat poison himself? Of course not. Someone else must have done that part – someone who would not have looked out of place in the kitchen. And I'll wager that same person kept watch at the library door while Culpin bricked up the fireplace.'

Mrs Rathborn looked disturbed by the idea. 'If you mean one of the staff, I cannot imagine who –'

'But how well do you really know them, Mrs Rathborn?' Aldo asked her coldly. 'Polly surprised you, didn't she?'

'Yes, but –'

'It's that reform-school girl,' growled Daniel. 'Sara Teltree. Once a felon, always a felon. I warned you, Mother, didn't I? We should never have employed her.'

'Hush, Daniel,' chided his mother. 'You of all people shouldn't be so quick to judge. Sara's a good Christian.'

'So who then?' Daniel challenged her, with a flash of his old fire. 'Alice? Nancy? Mrs Partridge? Williams? Mrs Haverhill? They're all good Christians, mother. But one of them is also a collaborator in murder!'

After lunch, Aldo and I retired briefly to our bedrooms. We were in the upstairs passageway, on the verge of returning downstairs, when we happened to spy Daniel Rathborn's chief suspect, Sara Teltree, limping slowly up the corridor towards us, a basket of fresh towels in her hands. We watched her slyly, like two crocodiles in a stream.

'Observe, Nathan,' whispered Aldo. 'Secrets weigh heavily on those frail shoulders. See the quick, guilty eyes, the white joints of those long fingers clutching the basket.

'Is she the one?' I muttered.

He shook his head. 'I don't think so. She knows something, though. Her fate is to find things, and she wishes it were otherwise, for it never does her much good. Call out to her, brother, as she passes.'

'Good afternoon, Sara!' I called.

'Afternoon, sirs,' she replied, scarcely breaking her stride long enough to curtsy.

'What troubles you, Sara?' asked Aldo.

'Nothing, sir,' she said, with the stare of a rabbit faced by a wolf. 'Do you mind if I put new towels in your rooms?'

She made to move past him and through the door, but was nearly tripped by his foot as it darted out to block her way.

'This must be a difficult time for you,' remarked Aldo conversationally.

She turned to him, visibly shaking.

'In–indeed, sir. It is for all of us.'

'And the difficulties will continue for as long as the cloud of suspicion hangs over the master,' he added. 'Which is why we must, all of us, confess to anything we know – anything, Sara! – that might help direct the authorities towards the truth.'

He looked at her sternly, but also sympathetically, and I must own that even I found myself drawn for a second or two into those brown eyes of his – deceptively soft they are, with their silky gold radiant lines, but his irises have a dark edge that I've always found dangerous, like something you might cut yourself on. As for Sara, she seemed to have sunk into a trance. The basket of towels had dropped from her nerveless hands and her little jaw had fallen open, as her own quick eyes (as grey as the scullery walls) became still and stared saucer-like into his.

She was brought to by a stringent bark from the landing. 'Sara!' called Miss Haverhill. 'Stop that staring at once, and get on with your duties.'

'Yes, oh yes, missus.' She grabbed up her basket, pushed her mob-cap back into place, and scurried into the bedroom.

'Gentlemen, welcome back,' bowed Mrs Haverhill. Her horsey, well-scrubbed face contemplated us with a mixture of mistrust and disapproval. It seemed that the housekeeper was as suspicious of loiterers in passageways as she was of comfortable furniture. Her sudden appearance on the landing was disquieting, and recalled Polly's characterisation of the woman as 'the unexpected creak on the stairs and the looming shadow in the hall'.

'I would thank you, young sirs, not to distract the maids from their duties,' she told us in a voice as harsh as the bristles on a scrubbing brush. 'They are easily distracted, and there is much work to be done. This household –'

'– won't run itself,' smiled Aldo. 'We are well aware of the helpless nature of this household, Mrs Haverhill.'

She nodded coldly, as if to say, 'You may think yourself clever, young man, but I have the measure of you.' Then she slipped out of sight.

We walked into Winterby village with Lily and Bonnie. It was a quiet, pretty little assemblage of streets and cottages, clustered around a steepled church built on a small mound. While the women wandered through the churchyard, Aldo and I went into the Old Cock Inn, a dark, cosy establishment of low beams, with a long bar, currently empty of patrons. The landlord was a thin, squinting fellow with a sandy moustache, who regarded us suspiciously as he wiped a glass. Aldo asked him for the address of the late Richard Culpin.

'You're not from the police?' he asked.

'Oh no.'

'Press then, are you?'

'Not at all,' I said. 'We're friends of the Rathborns, just visiting.'

'That family is cursed,' spat the landlord. 'Sorry to be blunt with you, sirs, but nothing good will ever come of their occupancy of that house. The sooner they sell up, the better for them and the better for this village.'

Tiring of the man's forebodings of doom, I asked again for the address, and he asked me why I wanted it. In truth we didn't have a reason deeper than curiosity, and I said so.

'Ah well, if you've come to gape, that's your business. We've had our share of gawpers and gapers these past few weeks, and I tell them all the same. He was never a good man, but he wasn't completely bad either, at least not until the Rathborns came and sent him packing. Something changed in him after that. And you sort of knew it would end badly – for him and for them.' The landlord replaced the glass he was holding on the shelf, slung the towel over his shoulder and leaned closer to us. 'And, you know,' he murmured, 'I don't think it's over. Culpin may be dead, but his curse remains, and will continue to remain for as long as the Rathborns choose to dwell in that house.'

Following the landlord's directions, the four of us found Culpin's cottage at the northern end of the village – one of a row of thatched dwellings facing a narrow road and a meadow.

'It is a very commonplace abode for such a monster,' was Bonnie's comment. She sounded almost disappointed, but was not mistaken in her description. The dark blue door and curtained windows in the brick frontage could not have presented a more unremarkable façade.

Aldo strode up and knocked at the door.

'Who do you suppose will be there?' Lily asked him.

'He may have had a tenant or a lady friend. It's possible they may know something.'

No answer was forthcoming, so Aldo slipped a previously written note through the letter box, and we departed.

Williams had lit a blazing fire in the drawing room on our return, and we sat before it, together with our hosts, taking tea and fruit scones brought in by young Sara. The girl lingered a while after she had poured and served. I saw a brief exchange of glances between her and Aldo before she finally hobbled out. A minute or so later, Aldo stood.

'Nathan,' he said. 'Show me that book you were referring to earlier on our walk.'

'Which book was that?' I asked, puzzled.

He frowned. 'The one about the girl who liked to *tell* all her secrets to a *tree*!'

'Ah, that one!' I said, finally understanding him.

We departed the room. Sara was waiting for us on the landing, superfluously dusting the leaves of a dying plant. When she saw us, she turned and began a quick, limping ascent of the second flight. We kept our distance as we followed her along the first-floor corridor. When she reached the end, Sara nervously turned to check that we – and only we – were behind her. Then she disappeared up the narrow, winding staircase that led to the servants' quarters in the attic. At the top of the stairs, we found ourselves in a dim, low-ceilinged corridor. Glimpses through the open doorways of its plainly furnished rooms showed sloping walls corresponding to the shape of the roofs. Sara stopped outside the third doorway on the right, and turned to us.

'This is Mrs Haverhill's bedroom,' she whispered to us. 'She sent me up here last Sunday morning to fetch her yellow scarf, which she needed as she was about to set off for church.' We followed Sara into the room. 'I found the scarf here,' she said, indicating the bed, 'and then my eye fell on this box.' She crouched down and pointed to a small chest beneath the bed. I wasn't sure exactly how her eye had 'fallen' on it, as it was placed a good way out of sight.

'I have these eyes that just see things, sir,' she said, as if reading my thoughts. 'I can't explain it.'

'It's your gift and your curse, Sara,' said Aldo, with some empathy.

'You are so right about that,' she nodded sadly.

'Did you look inside the box?' I asked.

'I didn't want to,' she said, flushing. 'I know this ability I have, this curse, only ever means trouble. Like when I found Polly's diary, sir, and then fervently wished I hadn't.'

'But you did look inside the box?'

She nodded.

'What's in there? What the devil did you find, Sara Teltree?' I stared at Aldo. 'Are we to presume Mrs Haverhill is caught up in all of this?'

Sara limped to the doorway. 'Do as your conscience guides you,' she said to us. 'I know nothing of that box. I was never here.' We listened to her uneven footsteps receding up the wooden passageway, and then clumping down the stairs.

Aldo glanced at me, then got to his knees and slid the chest out from beneath the bed. 'Keep an ear out for Mrs Haverhill, Nathan,' he said as he raised the lid. 'I swear that woman has the power to transport herself anywhere at will.'

I moved to the doorway and glanced into the empty passage, before peering over Aldo's shoulder to see what the box contained. He pulled out a pile of letters, which he pored over for a nerve-racking length of time.

'Make haste, brother,' I called. 'What have you discovered?'

'Well, well,' he said thoughtfully.

'What is it?' I cried.

'Letters from her aunt and from a friend in Hemel Hempstead and… one here from Richard Culpin.'

'Culpin?! Why would he be writing to her? What does he say?'

'It's dated third of May 1881. He writes: "Jane," – dear God, the woman has a first name!'

'Just read it, Aldo!'

'Sorry, yes. Here goes:'

I find it most gratifying to read your words of righteous ire as you catalogue the unspeakable indignities that the monster Rathborn has exacted upon you. As you well know, last winter, the same demon cast me from my home, your current place of employ, where it had pleased his father-in-law to have me reside as tenant, in perfect happiness and security, for some twenty years. And it was, I understand, with a similarly heartless impetuosity that he expelled you from his bed, to take up with that Irish trollop before even the scent of your mutual passion had faded from his sheets. It is a piteous tale, and one sadly common among those many I have spoken to who have fallen foul of

Rathborn's flint-hearted duplicity. But be strong, lady, and remember, you are not alone in the wrath you feel. Nurture it, let it smoulder within you, for a time will come, and surely soon, when we can work together in our mutual hatred and engender this vile ogre's just demise.

Yours, etc. Richard Culpin

'By Jove!' I said. 'Mrs Haverhill and Richard Culpin in a "mutual hatred" against John Rathborn. We have our collaborator, Aldo! She must have been the one who helped Culpin with the murders. Come quickly! Bring the letter. We should take it to the police!'

'Not so fast, brother,' he replied. 'This in itself proves nothing. We need to find a more recent communication, one with some hint of a plot, at least…'

'Hurry then,' I urged. 'Our absence downstairs will already have been noted.'

'Ah, here we are,' he said, extracting a letter from the pile in his fist. 'This one is dated some time in October 1882. I can't make out the precise date but it must have been around the time of the murders.'

Jane, I am most humbly obliged to you for your offers of assistance. My requirements are modest.

I ask only that each evening, before you retire, that you slide the cabinet in your office three feet to the left, leaving the trapdoor clear and enabling my admission to the house.

Yours, etc. Richard Culpin.

I removed my hand from my mouth, to which it had unconsciously become clamped as I listened to this startling epistle. 'We have it right there in your hands, Aldo,' I declared. 'What more proof do we need?'

'What… are you doing in my room?' The voice was like a steel blade being dragged across a whetstone.

I whirled around to see Mrs Haverhill at the far end of the corridor, staring at me as if at a spider she was about to trample. I could not imagine how she had materialised like that, at the top of a set of hollow wooden steps, without having made a single sound.

She marched up the corridor and turned into her room just as Aldo was rising to his feet, with the letters still in his hand and the chest open at his feet.

'That is private property, young man!' she bawled. Flecks of spit had appeared at the corners of her lips. Her head and upper body were rigid and erect, as always, but her hands were shaking.

Aldo remained surprisingly calm. 'It is also evidence of criminal activity,' he responded.

'You will give those letters to me this instant!' she cried, having apparently forgotten that we weren't a pair of housemaids to be ordered about at her pleasure.

Aldo pocketed the letters. 'Stand aside, Mrs Haverhill. Or do you want to add obstruction of justice to your list of crimes?'

For the first time I saw fear in her expression. She pressed her lips together and pushed a hand violently against her cheek to suppress a twitch that had started there. 'You have no right to do this,' she said.

'If you co-operate, Mrs Haverhill, things will be better for you,' I told her.

'I know what you're thinking, but you're wrong!' she said to me, and the cheek-quivering intensity of her stare – fanatical, defiant and terrified – was almost unbearable. 'I am *not* a murderer.'

'We'll see what the police have to say about that, shall we?' I said. 'Now stand aside, please.'

She continued to regard me with that fierce and desperate expression for some moments longer, before finally letting us pass.

14

n hour and a half later, almost the entire household gathered on the driveway below the front steps of Gravewood Hall. A chill breeze ruffled our coat collars and the lowering sun cast a silvery light upon the scene as we watched the young constable ushering a handcuffed Mrs Haverhill down the steps and into the waiting Black Maria. She looked straight ahead, her face impassive.

Inspector Simmons shook Aldo's hand and then mine. 'I want to thank you, young sirs,' he said, 'for your exceptional work in finding those letters. I cannot begin to fathom your methods, but the results speak for themselves.'

The plot to kill Mr John Rathborn and his hidden family had been exposed. The guilty parties were identified – one was dead, the other in the hands of the authorities. I felt a rare exhilaration as we walked up the steps and back into the house. In the entrance hall, I noticed that Mrs Rathborn appeared more serene than I had seen her in many weeks. She smiled and clasped my hand in both of hers. 'My dear young friend,' she said. 'How can I ever thank you for what you have done?'

I was charmed by her, as always, and quite struck by the return of warmth and vitality to her face. Yet, in all decency, I could not accept the compliments she wished to bestow. 'Thank Aldo,' I said. 'I was merely the witness this time.' I looked around for my brother, but could not at that moment locate him.

'I shall, of course, thank him too,' she said. 'You are both heroes. And now that justice has been served and Polly O'Brien and her little baby have been given decent Christian burials, I am quite sure the nights at Gravewood shall again be quiet and restful.'

A gust of cool air filled the hall. I turned to see the front door ajar and Aldo standing there on the veranda addressing a caller, a rather shabbily dressed young woman.

'Who is your brother speaking with?' wondered Mrs Rathborn. 'And where is Williams?'

'Beg your pardon, ma'am,' answered Williams, appearing at her elbow. 'I am not as fast as I once was, and the young master beat me to the door. He told me he would deal with the caller himself.'

Aldo closed the door and returned. 'It was nobody,' he said. 'A traveller seeking alms. I sent her on her way with a few shillings.'

I heard the soft clearing of a nearby throat and turned to see Daniel Rathborn looking at us with a rather embarrassed smile.

'Aldo, Nathan, I confess I misjudged you,' he said. 'You've both proved yourselves, well, thoroughly decent fellows. You stuck your necks out on my behalf – went the extra mile – which I didn't deserve after the way I behaved. Anyway… thanks and all that.'

'You're very welcome, Daniel,' I said

'I was wrong about Sara Teltree, wasn't I?'

'You were,' I nodded.

'Just out of interest,' he continued, 'how *did* you find out about those letters?'

As I opened my mouth to reply, Aldo's voice cut in. 'Luck, Daniel,' he said. 'Pure luck.' He winked at me. 'And luck is like lightning. You never can *tell* which *tree* it's going to strike.'

The supper table that night was a much happier place than on previous occasions. Wine was consumed in some quantity and I had rarely seen Daniel looking more cheerful. He laughed at Father's jokes and indulged Lily's impromptu lecture on the transit of Venus, an event which, she informed him, had taken place earlier that day. Astronomers had apparently made expeditions all over the world, to South Africa, Australia and Canada, to witness the passage of Venus across the Sun. 'This phenomenon,' she intoned reverently, 'will not occur again until the year 2004.'

Daniel looked suitably awed. 'It must surely be a good omen,' he suggested.

Lily, clearly disappointed with this response, replied: 'It is an astronomical event, sir, nothing more.'

Meanwhile, Mrs Rathborn and I chatted away very cosily at the other end of the table. I listened with interest as she relived some of her foreign adventures with her husband in the early days of their marriage. Before setting up his legal practice in London, he had been Deputy Queen's Advocate for the Northern Circuit of Ceylon, and he and Mary had lived in the colony for ten years during the 1860s. It surprised and pleased me to hear how warmly she spoke of her husband during that phase of their marriage. I was glad that she had, at least, some good memories to draw upon, and hoped, for her sake, that these would outlast her recollections of the squalid, loveless ending of their life together.

The only person who didn't appear to be enjoying himself was Aldo. He seemed withdrawn, saying little, and barely making the effort to partake in the conversations around the table. While Mrs Rathborn was conversing with Father, I took the opportunity to ask Aldo if anything was the matter. He leaned across the table and whispered: 'The unhappiness has not gone from this house. I fear the Rathborns will be disappointed, if they think this is the end of it.'

I was pondering what he could mean by this when I found Mrs Rathborn's attention once more upon me. She seemed extremely merry, and a little light-headed with wine. 'It's a shame,' she told me, 'that you never knew John when he was younger.'

'I've heard stories,' I said, 'from you and Father.'

'I loved him,' she said. 'In some ways, I still do.'

'You are very magnanimous,' was my response to this unexpected declaration.

There came a sudden, loud crash, as if a door had been slammed or a heavy object had fallen to the floor. I jumped, and turned, but saw nothing amiss in the room. To my astonishment, no one else seemed to have heard anything. Williams continued pouring wine into Mrs Rathborn's raised glass, and the conversation carried on between Father, Daniel and Lily, as if nothing had happened. Mrs Rathborn sipped her wine and gazed at me. 'Are you alright, Nathan?'

'Where's Aldo?' I said, noticing his empty chair.

'I have no idea,' she said carelessly.

Everything, I noticed, had turned a little odd. I was perceiving things differently to other people, as if I had become in some way unhitched from their world. I could hear their talk and their laughter, but it sounded muffled and not entirely comprehensible. 'I'm going to find him,' I heard myself say. But Mrs Rathborn had already turned away from me. As I rose to my feet, I noticed the edges of their bodies had blurred, as if viewed from behind thick glass. Only objects like the door and the furniture looked solid. I had not drunk anything stronger than water that evening, and I did not feel dizzy or sick – only distanced. I don't believe my departure from the table or the room was remarked upon, or even noticed.

In the hallway, I instinctively turned right, walking past the study and onwards to the library. I somehow knew Aldo would be there, or more likely below it in the secret room. The library was empty. The police had earlier closed up the false wall at the back of the hearth and moved the long table against the fireplace to act as a barricade.

A note pinned to the table warned in stark lettering: 'CRIME SCENE – KEEP OUT'. In the dim light, I perceived that the table had been pushed aside and the false wall reopened, uncovering the space behind, like the pitch-dark interior of a gaping mouth. I had no wish to go down there. Every nerve of my being flinched at the prospect, and yet I also knew I had no choice. That strange entreaty I had felt on my first night here, that whispery tremor on the air, that breathing piece of darkness, was calling on me again. I felt its desperation, and this time I could not ignore it.

I edged around the table, bent my head and eased myself into the hearth. I placed my foot on the scarcely visible first step, and thereafter, as absolute darkness cocooned me, I used blind touch, grasping the central stone column with my right hand as I made my descent. The column felt cool and reassuringly solid in a world that had recently slipped from its perch of certainty. It was my anchor in more ways than one and I gripped it with all my strength. An unsteady yellow light flickered into the stairwell from a crack beneath the wooden door at the foot of the steps. I reached into the blackness above it, and my fingers closed around the metal ring that served as a handle.

'Aldo?' I called. My voice sounded small and childlike.

'Come in,' came his reply. He was breathing hard as he spoke, as if tense.

At the sound of his voice, I shook desperately at the handle, making the iron latch clatter in its slot, until at last it freed itself and I burst in. Aldo stood there in front of me, facing into the candle-lit room, a strange gleam in his eyes. I turned to see what he was looking at. On the bed sat Polly O'Brien with her baby, looking as solid and real as any living being. She was seated on the side of the bed, with her feet on the floor. The baby was on her lap. Its mouth was wide open and its face was red, but I could hear no crying. Its arms and legs were rigid and its back and neck were arched. Polly was weeping as she rocked the child and kissed it. But she, too, did not make a sound. Helpless horror filled me as I took in this scene. I glanced at Aldo and, seeing his lack of response, I ran to the bed. I tried to pick up the child, but my hand connected with nothing. My legs became numb and I stumbled and fell backwards. Suddenly the air was rent by the infant's screams, and the muffled, jagged wailing of his mother. I closed my eyes and blocked my ears, but couldn't evade the sound. The babe sounded weak, close to death. When my eyes opened again, it was to witness a sight so awful that I quickly reclosed them. But the scene captured in my retinas mercilessly replayed itself: I saw Polly with her hands clasped around her little boy's neck, squeezing the life out of him. Her knuckles were white and her face was shaped in a scream of torment, as she roared and wept and grunted like an animal. Gradually, her dreadful noises faded. I peeped from between my fingers and saw the child lying still in her lap. The only sound that remained was Polly's breathing – loud, agitated breathing, as you might hear in a cell at Bedlam. And then, as she bent to kiss his little cheek, she emitted a soft moan. I had heard the sound once before, that night in the library. And again, the depth of its sadness bled into my bones and harrowed my soul. Finally, she looked up, and her eyes met mine. I looked into them – grey-green with hints of amber – and I had the odd and frightening sensation that, for the first time, she was actually seeing me, just as I could see her. There was no child in her lap now. She rose to her feet. The eyes that burned into mine seemed savage, deranged. Her mouth opened and my ears were punctured by a high scream. I crawled backwards, trying to get away from her, and I felt my back colliding with a heavy piece of furniture. A shadow fell across me, there was a loud smash, intense, crushing pain, and then everything collapsed into darkness.

CHAPTER

15

I awoke to a jolting sensation and the sound of swift hoofbeats. My lips were dry and my head was buffeted with waves of pain. I distinguished Aldo's lean, smiling face in the hazy foreground of my vision.

'Brother,' I croaked. 'Where? What?'

'Rest now, Nathan,' he said softly. 'We're on our way to hospital.' He raised a bottle to my lips and cool, life-saving water rained down onto my teeth and tongue. I slept some more.

The next time I awoke it was to bright sunlight pouring in from a window on the far side of a large white rectangular room. I was in a bed, one of many lining the two long walls. The pain in my head had subsided to a dull ache. I felt my forehead and encountered a bandage. A nurse in a white hat and long white apron appeared in the aisle between the beds. I called to her, and she came over to me.

'Mr Carter,' she said. 'I'm glad to see you've woken, sir.'

'Where am I?' I asked.

'You're in Hertford County Hospital,' she said, 'suffering from mild concussion. Would you like to see your family? They're just outside.'

'Yes, please,' I said.

A moment later, Lily, Father and Aldo came in. They looked pleased to see me, yet their smiles were subdued. Lily embraced me and I received warm handshakes from the men.

I had no memory of events immediately preceding my injury, and Aldo tried to enlighten me. 'A heavy wardrobe fell on top of you,' he told me. 'We were in the secret room, remember?'

I didn't. The recollection of that strange and frightening incident returned only gradually, over the following weeks.

'We've made some discoveries, son,' said Father. His face was grim, and he looked quite frail as he helped himself into a bedside chair, reminding me a little of his appearance in the months following Mother's death. I braced myself for disturbing news.

'Mrs Haverhill was not the murderer,' said Lily.

'She wasn't?' I gasped. 'Then who?'

Father cleared his throat and seemed about to say something, before thinking better of it. 'Perhaps it would be best if you heard the truth directly from Polly,' he said. 'When that wardrobe fell on you, Nathan, it revealed a hidden alcove in the wall behind it. On a shelf in the alcove, Aldo found a second diary. The diary is now in the hands of Inspector Simmons, but before we handed it over, I copied out the crucial final entry.' He reached into his pocket and pulled out a folded piece of paper, then settled his reading glasses on his nose. In a grave voice, he read out the following:

16 October 1882

Dearest diary, this is the happiest day of my life. Beg pardon for my messy scrawl, my hand is shaking so much with excitement for the news I have to tell, I can barely hold the pen. At long last my imprisonment in this hell-hole is nearing its end. Finally, my dearest wish, that I should marry J, is about to come true. I have just now had a visitor. Yes, I am not lying. I have had a visitor here in this room, and it wasn't J. Of all the people to visit – can you imagine? – It was the mistress. I cried out in shock when I saw her there at the door. But she came bearing a friendly smile and two plates of warm chicken stew. She told me that she is reconciled to our love and she will not stand in the way of a divorce. She asks for James and me to remain here one more night while she explains the situation to Mr D, and then we will be free to move upstairs and embark on the life I have dreamed of for eighteen long months. Arrangements still need to be finalised. It is probable that we shall need to move elsewhere, but that is of trivial concern when placed next to the heart-stirring prospect of a life spent in the fresh, open air alongside the man I love. I shall write some more about this anon, but now I must stop. My son is crying for his food.

'That is all there is,' said Father. 'She never wrote another word.'

'I don't understand,' I cried. 'Does this mean then that Mrs Rathborn knew about the secret room, and offered to divorce her husband? But that contradicts everything she told us.'

Father shook his head sorrowfully. 'Nathan, this visit from Mrs Rathborn happened on the 16th of October, the day after John Rathborn's death! Everything she said to Polly was a lie. And the plates of chicken stew were laced with rat poison.'

I sank back against my pillow, too stunned to speak.

'Other evidence has also come to light,' said Aldo softly. 'That woman who came to Gravewood Hall yesterday, who I claimed was a beggar, was, in fact, a lady who lived with Richard Culpin. She had found my note requesting information, and she came to tell me that Mrs Rathborn had visited their cottage on the afternoon of the 16th of October and had asked to speak with him. He never told her the nature of Mrs Rathborn's business with him, but it would be reasonable to assume that she had come to ask Culpin to brick up the library fireplace.'

'And last night,' said Lily, 'the police found a bundle of letters in Mrs Rathborn's possession, sent by Culpin. The letters threatened to reveal her dark secret unless she paid him regular amounts of money. The letters also said that he would "haunt" the house just to remind her that he wasn't going away.'

'But why?' I blurted, finding my voice at last. 'Why would she want to kill them? She didn't even love her husband.'

'Can you be sure of that?' asked Aldo. 'We both heard her reminiscing about Mr Rathborn last night, when the wine was acting on her, and a rather different picture of her feelings for him began to emerge, wouldn't you say? I think it's more likely that *he* fell out of love with *her*. But her love for him persisted, and eventually, after repeated betrayals, that love curdled into violent jealousy and hatred.'

'So she killed John as well?'

'There is no doubt about it,' said Father. 'The similarity of the crimes, and the timing, one after the other, point to a single murderer. In her jealous state, she probably took to spying on John's movements, and one night witnessed him entering through the secret door in the fireplace. It wouldn't have taken her long to establish what was going on, and then concoct her plan to do away with the three of them.'

'But if what you say is true,' I said, 'why was she so eager for us to come and investigate the noises? If she was guilty, she would hardly wish to draw attention to her crimes.'

'She was desperate,' said Lily. 'She was being harrassed by Culpin, and wanted him dead, but in a way that would not allow any suspicion to fall upon her. Then she remembered you, Nathan, and your famously volatile temper. Her plan was to invite you to Gravewood and lure you into a confrontation with Culpin. She hoped that Culpin would either be killed by you or hanged for your murder. Either way, her problem would be solved.

'Her interest in Aldo as a ghostfinder was entirely bogus,' said Father. 'She didn't actually believe her problem had a spiritual origin any more than Daniel did.'

'Her plan didn't work too well at first,' continued Lily. 'She hadn't expected you to faint with fear when you saw Culpin! So, the next night she armed you with a gun and, while Culpin was in the house, she faked a head injury, hoping this might rouse your chivalrous side sufficiently to go down and confront him. This time, as we know, her plan succeeded.'

'How can you be sure she faked that injury?' I said, trying not to sound too piqued (as usual, Lily had found a way of expressing herself that was very wounding to my pride).

'We can't be absolutely sure,' said Aldo. 'But we have to ask ourselves why she chose to come to your room and not mine. After all, my room was closer to the top of the staircase than yours. If she really was in a state of panic, having just suffered an assault, why did she not go to the nearest bedroom?'

I cast my mind back to that night and tried to recall my impressions of Mrs Rathborn when she came into my room. She had appeared genuinely scared, but then I, too, had been scared, and probably not very observant of details. She did, though, possess sufficient presence of mind to remind me to take my gun. When I mentioned this, Lily threw up her hands as if to say 'point proven'. 'What use would you have been to her without a gun?' she said in her charming way.

'But what she hadn't allowed for was the presence of a *real* ghost in the house,' said Aldo.

'That,' said Lily, 'is a matter of opinion! Mrs Rathborn was not undone by any supernatural phenomenon but by good old-fashioned detective work – wouldn't you agree, Aldo?'

'It certainly played its part,' he conceded.

I looked at Lily, Aldo and Father and shook my head. 'I was completely taken in by her,' I said.

'We all were,' said Father. 'And I was probably the biggest fool of all of us. In my defence, I have known Mary Rathborn for many years, and have always found her a fine, decent and morally upstanding woman. I can only imagine that John's persistent infidelities made her mentally unstable, and finally murderous. It frightens me that someone once so lovely could have committed such evil acts.'

'And you, Aldo?' I asked. 'Were you fooled by Mrs Rathborn?'

'I was,' he admitted.

'What first made you suspect her?'

'It was during the arrest of Mrs Haverhill,' he said. 'As I watched her being led away in handcuffs, I suddenly realised that she couldn't possibly be guilty.'

'Why ever not?'

'Well, do you remember that day when we interviewed Mrs Partridge, and she was telling us about her birthday? We were impatient with her at the time, but her anecdote turned out to be highly significant. You see, her birthday fell on the 15th of October, the day John Rathborn was poisoned, and

Mrs Partridge told us that, on that day, Mrs Haverhill couldn't wish her a happy birthday because she was away on a shopping trip. For some reason, that little snippet of information floated back into my head while I was watching Mrs Haverhill stepping into the Black Maria. It was instantly clear to me that she couldn't have poisoned the chicken stew because she hadn't been around to do it. And that set me thinking about who *had* been around that day – and I remembered Mrs Partridge telling us that Mrs Rathborn had come into the kitchen and smelt and tasted the stew. It occurred to me that, aside from Mrs Partridge, she was the only person with access to the stew at the crucial moment. Mrs Rathborn had told Mrs Partridge that they were dining out that evening, and indeed she and Daniel did dine out, but Mrs Rathborn knew that her husband would not be joining them, owing to his increasing reluctance to leave the house. So he was the only person to eat the chicken stew that night. By the time Mrs Rathborn and Daniel returned, John Rathborn was already dying of strychnine poisoning.'

'Ghastly,' I murmured. I was upset – more than I expected to be – by Mrs Rathborn's exposure as a conniving murderess, and her cynical exploitation of my family as a means of covering up her crimes. The pain had come back and I gestured to the nurse for another dose of morphine. Soon I was floating on a bed of warm sunshine, and the ache in my head, along with the sadness in my heart, began to subside.

I never saw Mary Rathborn again. It would have intrigued me, just once, to meet the real lady, with her mask of innocence removed, and to hear her story from her own lips, instead of contenting myself with the false and sensationalised accounts found in the popular press. As for her son Daniel, he was soon reinstated as senior partner at his firm, and to this day he continues to offer his legal services to my father.

Nothing ever came of the supposed romance I thought I had discerned taking shape between Daniel and Lily. She does not refer to him much these days, and I suspect, in the end, he failed to measure up to her image of what a husband should be. I stress that this is all pure conjecture. Officially, Lily remains appalled by the idea of marriage. Indeed, if I ever mention that a young man has asked after her, she unvaryingly declares her complete indifference to the said youth, and often as much as half an hour will then go by before she carelessly asks me to repeat word for word what the foolish young suitor had said.

Aldo continues, in his quiet way, to ponder the ripples in the ether, listening out for the cosmic undulations and speculating on what they might mean. He persists in clothing himself in a ludicrous manner, thinking only of what he likes and not how it works in combination. He rarely refers to the Rathborn affair these days, except to say that if he ever decides to set up a private detective agency, he would be sure to recruit young Sara Teltree, who he says is the most exceptional finder he has ever encountered.

In the spring of 1883, Gravewood Hall was sold to a local property developer. By all accounts, Daniel was not particularly happy with the sale price, although he could have little cause for complaint. Not only was the place run down, it had also acquired a sinister reputation. And, as Daniel later told me, once the stories had leaked out, its status as a haunted house quickly became established fact among potential buyers, no matter how many times he assured them that he had not seen hide nor hair of a ghost since the day his mother was hanged for murder.

ACKNOWLEDGEMENTS

I'd like to thank Mr Singer of Malorees Junior School for first inspiring my lifelong love of history, and my uncle Denis Judd, Professor Emeritus of History at London Metropolitan University, for our many fascinating conversations about the Victorians. I'm much obliged to Wilkie Collins for writing my all-time favourite Victorian detective novel, *The Moonstone*. Thanks also to my mother and father for their love and support and their helpful comments on earlier drafts of this book, and last but never least, thanks to my wife and best friend, P.

ABOUT THE AUTHOR

Alex Woolf was born in London in 1964. He has worked as a writer and editor for over 20 years and has published over 40 works of fiction and non-fiction, mainly for young adults. His fiction includes the *Chronosphere* series, a science-fiction trilogy published by Scribo, and *Soul Shadows*, an interactive e-novel published by Fiction Express. His short fiction has won or been shortlisted for several competitions. He lives in Southgate, North London, with his wife and two children. For the latest on Alex Woolf, visit www.alexwoolf.co.uk